Which Way is North?

All stories written by Chris M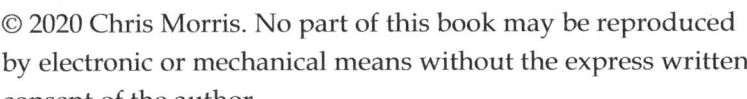

Book cover designed by Davi<

ISBN: 9798568428367

© 2020 Chris Morris. No part of this book may be reproduced by electronic or mechanical means without the express written consent of the author.

www.chrisamorris.com

www.facebook.com/ShortStoriesbyChrisMorris

www.twitter.com/chrismorris1982

Follow the "Short Stories by Chris Morris" podcast, available on all major platforms.

Which Way is North?

"Round here, we always stand up straight."
- Counting Crows, *Round Here*

*"It's only love, it's only pain,
It's only fear that runs through my veins,
It's all the things you can't explain,
That make us human."*
- Civil Twilight, *Human*

For Mirryn,

Because on a day that I had thought ordinary and dull, you said at end of it: "I wish the days with you didn't go so fast. This has been the best day ever."

Every day with you is the best day ever.

CHRIS MORRIS

Introduction

The following fifteen stories were all originally written during the Coronavirus outbreak in 2020. Even as I write this, there does not seem to be an end in sight to the pandemic. It's odd writing an introduction which mentions it not knowing whether it will be over by the time you the reader, have picked up this book.

It has been a difficult year for many, and not to toot my own trumpet of despair, but I have been affected by the monster of a year that is 2020 in more ways than some others. Firstly, writing is not my job – during the writing of these stories, I was a self-employed drum kit and percussion teacher. When lockdown was first put in place here in Scotland, I had to shut down my business and quickly learn to teach the vastly depleted numbers online instead. While all of this was happening, I experienced a heavy amount of tension between my daughter's mother and I in regards to access. I will not go

WHICH WAY IS NORTH?

into any detail about that in here, but I trust that you can understand that this was a very stressful situation. I also had a most major falling out with my own mother in regards to a brutal betrayal on her part, I couldn't see my girlfriend for several months because we didn't live together, and when lockdown was finally lifted, it wasn't long before we split up.

So an eventful year it has certainly been...

However, it has actually also been very positive.

I know, I know. It doesn't sound very positive at all. But something was happening during the course of writing these stories that was very beneficial to me and influenced not only the title of this book but indeed the actual production of it.

I hit rock bottom in 2020. And I believe that there is nothing else in this world that will motivate a person more than this. "Rock bottom" comes in many different forms for people, and for me, it was the aftermath of my breakup. I felt like I didn't have very much left at all – I didn't speak to my family, I had no real close friends, my job was actually a very lonely one and was at high risk of having to close, and there seemed to be no end to the tension between my daughter's mother and I, causing quite large amounts of distress for my daughter.

So I decided to improve my life. I decided to look for a new job, and I surprised myself by getting a good one very quickly. I decided to launch a podcast for my short stories (here's my first plug! Short Stories by Chris Morris, wherever you get your podcasts). I started improving my health and decided to resume running races. And I got really, really into my writing.

Nine of these stories were originally written before my own personal rock bottom, five after, and one during (I think it's self-evident which that one is…). They are presented here, not in order of when they were written, but in an order that I think flows nicely. I think it's good to present them a little scrambled because after all, life felt a little scrambled while they were written.

Most of these stories have been featured on my podcast (Short Stories by Chris Morris, wherever you get your podcasts). However, the versions here have been revised and extended. It was really nice, but also really challenging to revisit these different worlds and extend their stories a little. In some cases, I embraced the opportunity to give the story a fuller explanation to the reader, in other cases, I struggled to write in the same way I did when the story was first created because life moves on and feelings change.

These stories are all mixed in genre, and for me they represent things like struggle, feeling lost, trying to impress others and oneself, love, loss, happiness and perpetually attempting to find one's way. Hence the title: Which Way is North? We feel like we will have a clearer path through life once we really settle on knowing where we are going, and doing that requires finding our bearings. I think we all go through things like my own personal experience of 2020, and how we handle situations like these define the kind of people we are going forwards.

Since I'm not a famous author or one represented by an agent or publishing organisation, I hope you'll allow me a few shameless plugs on the next page…

CHRIS MORRIS

All of these stories (and more) are available to read in their original, unextended form on Reedsy Prompts — https://blog.reedsy.com/creative-writing-prompts/author/chris-morris/

My Facebook page is here –
https://www.facebook.com/ShortStoriesByChrisMorris

Twitter – https://www.twitter.com/chrismorris1982

Oh, and I almost forgot to mention, I also have a podcast. Just search "Short Stories by Chris Morris", wherever you get your podcasts.

WHICH WAY IS NORTH?

Contents

1. A Brief Account of a Paltry Portion (Being Merely One Part) of the Plenitude of Dreadful Affairs Which Plague the Daily Lives of the Human (And Sometimes Otherwise) Natives of Earlingdale Town   12

2. Big Feelings & Badington   35

3. The Grave of David Wilson   52

4. *Second Chances* Series 2 Episode 1: "The C Word"   72

5. *Second Chances* Series 1 Episode 2: "Back to School"   91

6. Is There Anybody Out There?   116

7. The Unlocking   128

8. Contingency Plan   150

9. My Hero   168

10. What If?   178

11. I've Been Thinking Blue   199

12. The Last Man Alive   210

13. Caroline   228

14. 50/50   246

15. Passing Places   261

CHRIS MORRIS

A Brief Account of a Paltry Portion (Being Merely One Part) of the Plenitude of Dreadful Affairs Which Plague the Daily Lives of the Human (And Sometimes Otherwise) Natives of Earlingdale Town

A chap came upon the door of the woodcutter as the timely night darkly settled into a crisp evening awaiting with apprehension the arrival of winter like a failing autumn leaf awaiting its drop unto the cold floor beneath.

That is to say, someone knocked at someone else's door on a cold autumn night.

The woodcutter, expecting no visitors and chiefly at this time of day, called out from behind his great wooden door before presuming to open it.

'Yes?' called he. 'Who be it rapping at me front door at a time such as this? What business do ye have?'

WHICH WAY IS NORTH?

'Hello sir,' came a foreboding voice from the other side of the door. It was a voice seemingly belonging to some dark creature of the night and no man at all. 'My name is Walter. How are your spirits this evening?'

'By spirits,' the woodcutter called. 'Do ye refer to me mood, or to t'ghosts kept in the jar in me kitchen?'

Being that the question was a good one and held much to consider, there was a moment's pause on the other side of the door before Walter spoke. 'Both,' he said.

The woodcutter said: 'I'm kept awake at night by ghostly moans accompanied by a feeling of trepidatious dread making the very air go as cold as Earlingdale Lake in t'winter. The spirits in the jar're fine mind. Now, what business have ye?'

'I am new in the neighbourhood, and I have simply come to introduce myself to you,' Walter said. 'Perhaps you could open your door so that I may see your face and we could palaver some?'

'That's a bad idea,' the woodcutter replied. 'There's bin speak of odd folk about: werewolves and vampires they say, no less.'

Walter chuckled softly. 'My dear fellow. If I were a werewolf, what would your disturbance with my presence here be? Hmm?'

The answer came quickly and plainly, as though it should have been obvious to Walter. 'That ye may rip out me throat and spit it into me fireplace so that every time me wife lights it she shall hear me last screams echo through the house and may it haunt her all her days.'

'Sir,' said Walter. 'A significant and well-founded concern that may have been if it weren't for one simple thing. I implore you to gaze out of your window and into the clear sky above, and if you would, tell me what you see there.'

Thereupon came some sighing and grumbling, accompanied by some thumping as the woodcutter manoeuvred himself to the nearest window, where Walter could see him peel back his curtains and look upwards.

'Well?' Walter asked brightly. 'What is it that your eyes can tell you about the night sky?'

WHICH WAY IS NORTH?

'Nothin' much,' the woodcutter said with a squinted eye pointed narrowly upwards. 'Same as always. Stars and the moon.'

'What kind of moon?' Walter inquired.

'Crescent,' the woodcutter said. 'Or I don't know me oakenwood from me wife's frock.'

'Indeed,' Walter said. 'And pray, tell me what kind of moon would implore you to watch out for werewolves?'

The woodcutter turned and eyed Walter out of his window now. 'Aye, alright. But who's to say yer not a vampire?'

'I *am* a vampire,' Walter simply returned.

'Heathen!!' the woodcutter cried. 'Foul thing from the depths of hell! Begone, or so help me I'll…'

Walter calmly raised a hand. 'Now, now! Please be civil. I am required by the mayor of Earlingdale to make myself known to my new neighbours. I have done as instructed. I'd rather you and I could be friendly with each other.'

'*Friendly!?*' the woodcutter cried in disbelief. 'How do I know yer not going to change yerself into a bat and fly into me house to suck me blood until there's nowt left?'

'I must say,' Walter said, remaining as calm as the flame from a candle burning in a windless room. 'I don't appreciate racist remarks such as these. I am a *vampire*, yes I suck the blood from innocent and peaceful civilians and damn their souls to a miserable afterlife in hell for all eternity, but I *cannot* turn into a bat. Viscous rumour.'

'Well, in any case,' the woodcutter continued. 'We don't want *your* sort round 'ere. Trouble'll come of it, mark me words. Might see if I can't have a word with the mayor meself.'

Walter remained remarkably calm, irritated as he was by this man's unwelcoming and impolite attitude. 'Look, sir. If you just remain indoors at night you'll be fine; I can't come out during daylight, as I'm sure you well know. The mayor has already given his approval for my residency here so your argument will fall on deaf ears, I'm afraid. There's no reason you and I can't be friends.'

The woodcutter, aghast, dropped his mouth open. 'No reason? No reason! P'raps we can't be *friends*, sir,

WHICH WAY IS NORTH?

because the moment me back's turned to ye, yer fangs'll find the side o' me neck!'

'You'll have to be on your guard, I concede,' Walter said.

'On me guard!?' the woodcutter hissed. 'Now you listen 'ere, vampire. This town has had enough o' the likes o' you and yer sort. We don't want no vampires, werewolves, zombies, ghouls or goblins o' *any* sort 'ere. Just las' year we had a shapeshifter eat poor ol' Fatty Bainwright. Disgusted itssel' as a grand cake an' when ee went over to inspect it, it swallowed im up whole.'

'Monsters are people too,' Walter said. 'But seeing as there doesn't appear to be any reasoning with you, I'll bid you a good evening and be on my way.'

The conversation concluded, Walter sauntered serenely away from the woodcutter's house. Even as he did, he heard the man call to his wife.

'Bridget! Let's have mutton for tea! And put plenty o' garlic in it!'

How very discourteous, Walter thought.

***

A rap similar in nature and equal in vigour came upon another door on the succeeding morn betwixt Lake Earlingdale and the town hall some length from the woodcutter's dwellings on a day clear and bitter as a fresh and thin slice of lemon.

That is to say, the next morning someone else knocked on someone else's door on the other side of Earlingdale.

The door to the cottage, which happened to be owned by a hunter of great renown, opened more widely than that of the woodcutter's door, being that the hunter feared very little in the way of man or beast. Standing in front of the woodcutter was a large man with a great beard, unkempt and unwashed. He made no eye contact with the hunter, his eyes remaining instead fixed upon a faded piece of parchment grasped in both hands.

'Hello,' the man read in a mechanical sort of manner. 'My name is Joseph, and I have just made… erm… I can't read the next word…'

'Spell it,' the hunter helpfully suggested.

Joseph squinted at the parchment. 'A… C… C… O… M… M…'

WHICH WAY IS NORTH?

'Accommodation?' the hunter asked.

'Tha's the one,' Joseph said with gratitude. 'I have just made *accommodation* in one of the cottages betwixt the town hall and Lake... Sorry, I can't read the nex' one either.'

'Earlingdale,' the hunter said.

Joseph looked up at this, bewildered. 'How did ye know that? I didn't even start spellin' it! Yer not a witch are ye? I'm not livin' nex' door to a spellcaster!'

The hunter, perplexed by the foolishness and absurdity of the accusation and eager to move the conversation to its conclusion, shook his head. 'Ye don't get *man* witches. Least not in these parts. Now go on.'

Joseph returned his eyes to the parchment. 'I have been *in-struc-ted* by the mayor of... erm...'

'Earlingdale,' the hunter said, and motioned with his hand for Joseph to continue.

'Aye, Earlingdale,' Joseph said. 'To inform you that I am a... Blast it I can't read this one neither.'

'Spell it,' the hunter said with a roll of the eye and a deep sigh.

'W... E... R... E... W... O... L... F.'

The hunter stood upright and suddenly on his guard. 'A *what!?*'

'I dunno,' Joseph said. 'What's it spell?'

'A damned beast of the night!!' the hunter shrieked. 'A murderous miscreation spawned from the devil hisself!! A moon howler!!'

'Oh,' Joseph nodded. 'It says werewolf. Course it does.'

'Now you listen 'ere!' the hunter said, pointing an aggressive finger towards Joseph. 'We don't want yer sort round 'ere. A hunter as renowned as me, this town has seen to rely on me for everything from killin' banshees to trolls. Paid handsomely for it I was too. But me next door werewolf neighbour, I'll kill for free.'

'What sort o' welcome is that for yer new neighbour?' Joseph asked, aghast.

'You *ain't* welcome!' the hunter returned.

'Look 'ere!' Joseph cried. 'I've got *rights* same as any man. It's not my fault I was tricked by a gnome into drinkin' a magical potion that he said was to make me filthy rich an' handsome.'

WHICH WAY IS NORTH?

'Ye fell for a gnome scam?' the hunter asked with a certain amount of conceit. 'Everyone knows the ol' bait n' switch. It's usually a sleepin' potion they'll give ye though – so they can rob ye o' yer fortunes.'

'Aye, well,' Joseph said with little shame. 'Seems someone slipped this gnome a werewolf potion. Bad luck for him – he gave it to me on a full moon, rest his little soul.'

'Well, in any case,' the hunter said, attempting to bring the conversation back on point. 'I can't promise ye I won't use me musket on ye. Got to keep meself and me family safe. I'm sure ye'll understand.'

'Oh, that reminds me,' Joseph said. He fumbled around in his jacket pocket for a moment before producing another small piece of parchment which he handed to the hunter, who upon taking it from the werewolf and reading it became irate once again.

'Orders from the *mayor!?* Nobody is to harm Joseph the werewolf while he remains in human form. Only once he has transformed into his wolf state, and *only* if your life is in peril may you use force to subdue – *not kill* – under penalty of death by hanging!'

'I like yer mayor,' Joseph said, and then added with a chuckle: 'Well, *our* mayor. He's very... what's that word in... in...'

'Inclusive,' the hunter said. 'Aye well he can *include* my name on what I'm sure will be a substantial list of complainers from this town.'

'I have to say,' Joseph said. 'This is the worst welcome I've received in a place since I was chased out o' West Yarlington by a crowd o' villagers carrying silver pitchforks! They needn't o' had the silver blades, I was in me human form, but I was unimpressed all the same. If I've got to write to me union representative to solve this, I will.'

'*Union!?*' the hunter exclaimed. 'Wha' union?'

'The Society of Defenders for Folk of Magical or Unwanted Dark Properties,' Joseph said. 'Stood by me for these last six years. Even when I ripped the head off one o' their members during a meetin' we accidentally scheduled for a night with a full moon. Silly mistake. Ye live and learn.'

'There's a *union* for filth like you!?' the hunter said with an expression akin to one who has, upon intending to take a large bite out of an apple has instead sunk his teeth into a peeled lemon.

'Right,' Joseph said hotly. 'I'm goin' to be the bigger man an' walk away. I've done me duty by the mayor. If ye've never lived next door to a werewolf before here's my advice: jus' take a holiday once every month, during the night o' the full moon. Ye should be fine unless I catch a good whiff o' yer scent. If ye want, I've made scones. Drop by any time.'

***

Word having extended out to the most of the folk of Earlingdale as swiftly as a starving man who remains particular about his bread being buttered to the very edge may briskly scatter that butter, it was demanded of the mayor to call an immediate town meeting. The hall was stuffed to the brim with people to the point where, had the unfortunate Fatty Bainwright's shapeshifter still been alive to see, it would have smacked its lips greedily and waited outside for a feast.

Presently, the deputy mayor stood and raised a hand to signal his desire for silence.

'Ladies and gentlemen o' Earlingdale,' he said. 'We are called 'ere to this meetin' by a desire, great in nature an' urgent in appearance, by many o' ye to discuss the matter o' the appearance o' dark creatures in this town.'

'Dark *folk*,' one citizen, Jasper the twine maker piped up to correct, and there was much grumbling in disapproval at this. 'Now come on, let's use their proper term's all I'm sayin'. We've all got to live together, so let's not be too rash in our attitude t'wards them.'

Suddenly, and without any hesitation or surprise from those around him, another of the townsfolk bolted up from his seat and spoke. 'I motion that we throw Jasper the twine maker out o' this meetin'! All in favour?'

There was a loud, enthusiastic call from those in the hall: 'AYE!!!'

'All opposed?' the speaker asked.

Barely heard among the silence was a feeble 'erm… me?' from Jasper before he was forcefully and vigorously ejected from the hall.

'Right,' the deputy mayor said. 'Well, that settled…'

WHICH WAY IS NORTH?

'Now wait jus' a minute,' the woodcutter who had previously been visited by a vampire said. 'Where's the mayor? We asked to speak to him, not his deputy.'

'Ah,' the deputy said with a raised finger. 'Unfortunately he's bin called away on important business with the mayor of Cheffingvale.'

The hall erupted in much anger with many raised voices.

Important business!?

Cheffingvale!?

This better not be like the time ee was off on the "important business" o' comparing sizes o' parsnips wi' the mayor o' West Yarlington!

The deputy was eventually able to calm the folk of the meeting and continue their conversation. 'Now let's try an' be as civil about this as we can manage. I appreciate we're all feelin' a little passionate this evening but let's try t'get our points across calmly an' listen t'one another. Now, we're here t'discuss the concerns o' many of ye about particular new constituents o' this town. Who would like t'speak first?'

Hereupon several folk stood up at once and again there was much shouting and even some pushing at each other which in one case turned into a fistfight that some tried to stop while others took advantage to place bets. When someone was finally able to speak, it was the hunter who had been visited by the werewolf who did so.

'I've had *enough,*' said he. 'I've had it up t'*here* with defendin' this town from the likes o' these monsters. An after all t'work I've done fendin' off all sorts o' the devil's children, our mayor chooses t'reward me by sendin' a bloomin' *werewolf* t'live nex' door! I want im *out* o' there immediately. He can go an bother someone else!'

'Now jus' hang on a second there!' another of the townsfolk argued. "Ye want t'send this werewolf o' yours to another part of Earlingdale? Wha' makes *you* so special that ye have the right t'send a werewolf t'someone else's door, eh?'

'I'm the greatest hunter this town has ever seen!' the hunter proclaimed. 'If it weren't fir me, yeh'd all be either starved or slaughtered by now!'

At this, another of the meeting attendees stood and projected: 'Greatest this town has seen!? Me great-

great-grandfather has a *paintin'* done o' 'im on the wall o' this very buildin' for slayin' the great basilisk! How many serpent kings have *you* killed, I wonder?'

'Yer great-great-grandfather did no such thing!' the hunter asserted. 'The snake swallowed im whole an' choked to its death on im! Hardly the stuff o' heroes an' legends!'

Once again the hall became immersed in squabbling and bickering, the deputy mayor tried once or twice to raise his voice above it but failing to do so, chose to sit down and place both hands over his face in hope that the townsfolk would settle themselves.

Previous to the conclusion of the congregation and the securing of the town hall for the evening, a request (which was granted) was made to the deputy mayor that one of the members of the meeting could make lodgings there for fear that upon arriving at his own home he may be subject to his neighbour's dark work of the night, being that the sun had long set and the night was as dark as the spirit of a humourless ghoul endlessly haunting the wide world.

That is to say, the woodcutter chose to sleep in the town hall instead of going home and facing the possibility of encountering Walter the vampire.

***

Being that the townsfolk of Earlingdale made no attempt to suppress their looks of scorn as they passed Joseph in the marketplace or on the streets, and being that tonight was the last before the next full moon, the werewolf decided to freely take a slow walk in the woods on the other side of town.

The crisp and colourful autumn leaves crunched satisfactory underfoot, and Joseph heard no other sound besides the occasional flutter of a night bird or bat overhead, and the branches of the trees swaying gently as the cold breeze whispered through them. As he walked, he enjoyed thoughts of what he was going to cook for dinner, causing his stomach to grumble. He became slightly disturbed as thoughts of human flesh became mixed in with fantasies of vale stew, but with a shrug of the shoulder and an admission to himself that these thoughts were only natural being that he had now been

WHICH WAY IS NORTH?

living as a werewolf for some eight years, he continued his walk merrily.

A flutter among some of the branches above brought into his view one of the bats he'd been hearing. He watched it now as it gracefully sailed through the brisk air and turning, came in flight back towards Joseph. Preparing to duck (as it looked as though the bat had somehow lost its bearings and was like to crash awkwardly into his head), Joseph watched a most peculiar sight: as it neared him, the bat grew larger and swiftly turned before Joseph's very eyes into a tall, thin and pale man who now purposely crashed into him, and pinning him to the forest floor, bared his long white fangs and prepared to sink them deep into Joseph's neck.

To both the werewolf and the vampire's surprise, Joseph chuckled. 'A vampire! Yer jus' like me!'

Pausing in his assault and confused by this statement, the vampire looked all around the face of Joseph before saying: 'You are no vampire...'

***

The odd pair sat side by side on one of the wooden benches close to the middle of the forest and discussed the troubles of being a creature of the night in a town largely unaccepting of such folk.

'I must feed, like anybody else,' Walter lamented. 'The deer of this forest do not show any objection to the presence of humans in their dwellings, yet are they not hunted? And yet do the human children not cry out in joy to see one galloping through the trees?'

'Exactly!' Joseph agreed. 'It's jus' once a month I'm found to be on the prowl. The rest o' the time could be spent in friendship. Aye, I migh' rip out yer throat one night, but that's not the *real* me. I don't get the chance to show the real me. It's all *silver bullets* this an' *burned at the stake in yer human from* that.'

'Stake!' Walter gasped. 'Don't mention stakes! I'm threatened by one of those nearly every day. *I'll drive a stake through your heart as you sleep during the day* they say. I mean, can you imagine if I went about my day telling them all that I'll be drinking their blood as soon as their backs are turned? The outrage it would cause!'

'I had a friend once,' Joseph said. 'He was a normal sort o' man, the way I was b'fore me wolf days. Popular man; the townsfolk loved im and would all trust im with their lives. Anyway, he tragiclly died o' an accident.'

'I'm sorry,' Walter said. 'How did he die?'

'Well, he was the town executioner,' Joseph began. 'An he was also in charge o' trainin' the new executioners in how to use the equipment. He was demonstratin' to one of the new boys how to place the noose over t'neck. He had it in place an then he said: "An this is where ye'd shout to yer lever boy: *pull the lever!*" Only thing was, a new lever boy was gettin' trained that day too an ee heard the call and did as ee heard.'

'Oh, how terrible,' Walter said.

'Aye, well thing is,' Joseph said. 'He came back as a zombie. Dunno how it happened but over t'moon I was. But the townsfolk weren't happy. Cut his head off, so they did.'

'Even though he was so beloved before!' Walter gasped. 'That's terrible!'

'Aye,' Joseph agreed. 'An it didn't stop there neither. He came back once again, this time as a poltergeist. The townsfolk had the bishop come'n do an exorcism. It's like they all jus' up and forgot how much they used t'like the man.'

The conversation was interrupted by a sudden rush of footsteps, and looking slightly to their left, the vampire and the werewolf observed the woodcutter and the hunter as they rushed forwards with a stake and a musket (no doubt containing a silver bullet despite his human form, Joseph thought) respectively. Neither Walter nor Joseph made any attempt to defend themselves, for they saw that within the shadows a mere foot away from the rushing humans was all the protection they needed.

The humans were stopped by a tall figure which shot spikes out from within its wrists, swiftly penetrating the backs of their heads. They dropped their weapons and indeed collapsed to the floor of the cold forest, lifeless. After a moment where it appeared to be somehow feeding on the downed pair, the tall figure shortened its spikes and walked calmly towards Walter and Joseph.

'Good evening,' Walter greeted. 'It's good to see a wraith in action.'

WHICH WAY IS NORTH?

The wraith smiled, and observing that Walter was sitting affably with Joseph remarked: 'Ah, I see the two of you have met. Very good.'

'Aye, albeit we nearly had a misunderstandin' upon our meetin',' Joseph said with a smirk. 'Almos' had two holes in the side o' me neck. Is it possible to be a vampire *and* a werewolf d'ye think?'

The trio laughed heartily. Indicating towards the human pair on the floor ahead of them, Walter asked: 'What will come of them?'

'They'll be like me soon,' the wraith said. 'And then I'm sure we can convince them to join our cause.'

'Aye,' Joseph said. 'We'll turn all of Earlingdale into a town made for people like us. Never have to convince people it's okay to have someone the likes o' us living next door t'them again.'

'Because they *will* be us,' Walter agreed enthusiastically.

'Yes,' the wraith said. 'In time, we will make that dream come true. Now if you'll excuse me, I'm going to make myself scarce before anyone happens upon us. We don't want too many questions, do we?'

CHRIS MORRIS

'No, of course not.' Walter said. 'We'll be on our way too. Speak to you again very soon, Mister Mayor.'

WHICH WAY IS NORTH?

Big Feelings & Badington

'I don't know why I feel like crying, Daddy, I just do.'

Even as I said the words, I could feel my eyes getting wet, and my lower lip begin to shake. I was feeling sad and I only knew a little bit why, so I didn't tell my Daddy anything. He would probably ask lots of questions that I didn't know the answer to, so I just told him I didn't know. It was easier.

'It's okay honey,' he said. 'Sometimes people feel like that. You're only five, and you have a lot of big emotions to deal with.'

'What's *emotions?*' I asked, hoping I was pronouncing it properly.

'Feelings,' my Dad said. 'Like happy and sad, or scared, or angry. Do you feel sad?'

I paused for a moment, thinking about it. I thought about my Mummy, and how she never wants to talk about Daddy, and how Daddy never wants to talk about her either. That made me sad. I didn't know if they liked each other, even though I was sure they both loved *me*. I didn't really know who to talk to about it.

'Molly?' Dad said. 'Did you hear me? Do you feel sad?'

'Kind of,' I said. I didn't look at my Dad.

'Why?' Dad asked.

'I don't know!' I said in an irritated tone. 'I just do.'

'Okay,' my Dad said. 'You know, you can talk to me about *anything*. If you figure out what's making you sad, it might help to tell me.'

'Yeah, I know,' I said.

'Okay, Molly,' Daddy said, and he kept driving the car.

We had been on the road for a long time now. Dad gave me one of those sweeties before we left; the orange flavoured ones that make sure you don't feel sick in the car. I ate it at Lucy's house before we left. She had found some at the shops for me because Daddy didn't know where to find them. Lucy was really excited about today. She was driving the other car, the one with Sophie and her Dad in it. Sophie was Lucy's *neece,* and she said that

WHICH WAY IS NORTH?

Lucy was my Daddy's *girl friend.* I didn't really know what a *girl friend* was, but I thought it was someone special.

'Do you know that your Dad and my Auntie Lucy are in love?' Sophie had asked me once.

'What does that mean?' I had asked.

Sophie had just giggled.

'Is Sean okay?' my Dad asked me.

I looked over at the car seat beside me. Sean was sleeping. He was almost the same age as me and Sophie, and Lucy was his Mum. I didn't know who his Daddy was, but sometimes people thought that *my* Daddy was his Daddy, and sometimes they thought that Lucy was my Mummy too. I didn't know why. It was silly.

'Yeah,' I said to my Dad. 'He's just sleeping.'

We passed lots of fields with animals in them. My Dad pointed them out each time. I saw cows, sheep and loads of birds. I loved animals. The cows were the cutest. I saw them eating grass and looking at our car. I wondered what they were thinking about it; if they knew what a car was, and if they could see us inside. I wondered if they wished they were in a car, or if they thought they would be scared to be in one because it goes so fast.

'Daddy?' I said as loud as I could; we had our windows open, and the noise of the wind combined with the music my Dad had on made it hard to talk.

'Yeah, Molly?'

'How come everyone's having two sleeps at the cottage except us?'

My Dad turned his head to look at me briefly with a sad kind of look on his face before he turned round to look at the road again. He reached a hand back and patted my leg a little.

'I told you,' he said. 'Your Mum wants you back tomorrow night.'

'Could you not ask her if I could stay for longer? Because it's special?' I asked.

My Dad had a funny look on his face then. It was a look I hated. I hated it because he did it every time I asked him a question that he didn't know the answer to. I hated it because I thought it meant he was sad. I hated it because I felt like it was my fault he was sad. He didn't have to answer the question though; he got interrupted

WHICH WAY IS NORTH?

by something else. A big house at the end of a tiny, little road up ahead.

'Here we are! Wow, it's really nice, isn't it?'

My Daddy smiled as he drove the car towards it. When we got closer, I saw that Lucy's car was already there, and I saw Mike standing outside the big house. Mike was Sophie's Dad. They were all one family; Mike, Sophie, Sean and Lucy. Me and my Dad were a different family, with different last names, but sometimes Sophie said we were all like one big family anyway.

Sophie came running out towards our car when she saw us, smiling and full of energy. She came to my window and jumped up so she could see me.

'Molly! How *cool* is this place! There's a duck pond! And we have our own room! With bunk beds!!'

The others came over to see us too, and my Dad took all of our stuff from the car into the house.

'I think we'll have a really nice time here,' Dad said.

***

I was tired the next day because the first night in the cottage was really fun. Me and Sophie stayed up late (our

Dads said we could, but then we stayed up even longer than we should have). We played loads of fun games, and Sophie kept making me laugh. I had to try really hard not to laugh too loud because I knew Dad would hear us, and he would try to make us go to sleep. Sophie fell asleep first; she let me have the top bunk bed because I wasn't going to be here the second night anyway, so she could choose whatever bed she wanted. When she said that, I felt a little bit like crying again, but the feeling went away as soon as I started laughing again.

We woke up quite early, even though we were a little bit tired. We got a special breakfast; croissants with chocolate spread and really yummy orange juice. It had bits in it that were even juicier when you chewed them. I loved it.

We saw the ducks. Lucy said it's not so good to feed them bread, but she brought along some peas to feed them with. My Dad managed to get one of the ducks to eat some out of his hand instead of throwing them onto the ground. I wanted to try it too so my Dad told me to hold both my hands open and make a sort of bowl. He poured some of the peas into my bowl and one of the

WHICH WAY IS NORTH?

ducks (a lady one, it was brown) came over and took some from my hands. Its beak felt funny and I was a little scared it was going to hurt me by accident, so I spilled the rest of the peas. The little duck looked happy enough about this and ate up the rest from the ground.

After that we played a game around the back of the house that was a bit like tennis, but I kept forgetting what it was called.

'It's *bad-min-ton,* Molly,' Mike was telling me.

'Badington,' I tried.

'Almost,' my Dad smiled.

We had a round where it was children against grown-ups, which was really fun. We would have won if it wasn't for Lucy being so good at it. My Dad and Mike weren't very good; they kept missing the ball every time they tried to hit it. Lucy finally had enough and shouted at my Dad one time, but they ended up laughing and then kissed on the lips.

'*Eewwww!!*' Sophie shouted, covering her face with her hands. 'They just *kissed!!*'

I didn't know what was so disgusting about it. My Dad kissed me all the time. Not on the lips though. Me and Lucy were the only people I saw him kiss, and I wondered if he kissed anybody else. I didn't think he did. I wondered why Sophie made such a big deal out of it.

The day was really hot again, even hotter than yesterday. My Dad put sun cream on me, and I liked the smell of it. It made my arms and legs go all slidey. We had some more tasty orange juice (but different from the one we had at breakfast), and it helped us to cool down. Sean drank all of his up really quickly and then started crying because there was none left.

We all went out in the cars after our lunch and took our swimming stuff with us. There was a river not far away that came into a big bit of water that looked just like an outside swimming pool. There were rocks to the side of it that were good for jumping off. Mike was the first one to do it, and Sean didn't seem scared of it at all, even though he was smaller than me and Sophie. All of us children were wearing armbands to help us float in the water, but the grown-ups didn't need any.

I didn't jump in, but when I put my foot in the water, I discovered that it was really, really cold. I drew my foot back quickly and screamed a little bit.

WHICH WAY IS NORTH?

How could it be so cold!?

When Sophie tried it, she thought it was cold too. She screamed loudly, but then she started laughing. She took my hand and said that we should walk in together. I thought it was funny, but it was still hard to get inside the pool because it was so freezing. We eventually got all the way in but by the time we did, we were laughing so hard we could hardly speak. Once we were in the water, we warmed up and it wasn't so bad. We stayed in the shallow bit and watched the grown-ups jumping off of the big rocks and trying to stop Sean from following them. He was brave, but still too little to be doing those big jumps.

On the way back to the cottage, we stopped at a shop for some ice cream, and we ate it outside in the sunshine. The ice cream was really tasty and helped us to cool down in the hot day. By this time, a gentle wind was blowing too, and it was nice to feel it on my face.

It was just me and Dad in our car on the way back to the cottage again, and my mind started wondering about things, so I thought I would ask about them.

'Daddy?' I piped up over the noise of the wind rushing through the window.

'Yeah?' he said.

'Does my Mummy not want me to see you?'

One more time, Dad's face went funny, and he had a big sigh. 'No. I don't think she wants that.'

'What do you mean you don't think?' I asked.

'Your Mum loves you,' Dad said. 'Maybe she just loves you so much that she wants to have you at hers for longer.'

'But you love me too,' I said.

Dad looked at me in his mirror a little bit. His face looked quite sad again. 'Of course I do, Molly.'

'Why do you not say that you want me to come to yours more then?' I asked.

'Your Mum knows I want you more,' Dad said. 'It's just really complicated.'

'What does *complicated* mean?'

Dad paused a bit again. It seemed like he was trying to find the right words to say. 'Something complicated is something that's either hard to explain, or has too many things to talk about.'

WHICH WAY IS NORTH?

There was a silence between us for a little while then. Dad had been singing along to his music, but he wasn't now. I wasn't even sure if he was actually listening to it.

'Do you and Mummy not like each other?' I asked.

He looked at me in the mirror quickly again. 'We don't love each other. But we both love you, and that's all that really matters, isn't it? And now you've met lots of new people that you love, like Lucy, and Adam. And that wouldn't have happened if me and your Mum still lived in the same house.'

Adam lived with me at my Mummy's house. I wondered if that meant that my Mum was Adam's *girl friend*. I thought maybe I would ask her.

'I'm going to tell my Mummy I want to come to your house more,' I said.

'Oh, Molly,' Dad replied. 'You don't have to do that, honey. I think your Mum knows. And she knows that I want to see you more too.'

'How do you know?' I asked.

'Well, I got a letter about it,' Dad said.

'From my Mummy?'

'No,' Dad said. 'Not from her. Well, I suppose it *was* in a roundabout sort of way.'

'What do you mean?' I asked.

Dad sighed again. 'Nothing, Molly. It's okay. Just some grown-up stuff that's hard to explain. You're happy when you're with me, and you're happy when you're with your Mum, aren't you?'

I nodded, but my voice went quiet. I had a sad feeling that I felt in my heart and in my tummy. It was hard to know really *why* I felt like this. Maybe it was *complicated.* I cheered up a little when me and Dad started playing I-Spy and fining lots more of the animals we'd seen the day before.

Once we got back to the cottage later, I was feeling really tired. Mostly because I should have slept earlier the night before, but I was just so tired from all the fun we'd been having.

'Can me and Sophie go and play in the bedroom?' I asked my Dad.

'Yes,' he said. 'But remember we'll have to get going really soon, okay?'

WHICH WAY IS NORTH?

I had forgotten about that. My heart sank, and now I didn't want to go and play so much, because I knew it would be over soon. I think Mike saw how sad my face must have looked because he said something quietly to my Dad.

'Would have been nice of her Mum to let her stay with you one extra night for once. Isn't asking much, is it?'

I looked over at my Dad. He looked really sad.

'Ssshh!' Lucy hit Mike in the shoulder, then turned to me. 'Go and have some fun with Sophie, Molly. We'll shout on you when it's time to leave.'

***

On the drive home, me and Dad were both really quiet. I looked out the window and saw loads of animals. Dad pointed some of them out at first but then didn't say anything after a while. We didn't play any I-Spy.

I wished we could have stayed at the cottage for one more night. I wondered what Sophie and Sean and Lucy and Mike were doing. I imagined them feeding the ducks again or playing *Badmanting*. I was a little bit sad thinking about it.

Then I looked at my Daddy and thought that he looked sad too. And I wondered if he was sad thinking about them all back at the cottage, and if he wished he was there too. I wondered if he was angry about it.

'Daddy?' I said.

'Mmm?' Dad sounded.

'Are you angry at me?'

He looked around briefly. His expression was puzzled.

'No,' he said. 'Of course not. Why would I be angry at you?'

'Because you have to leave the house,' I said. 'Because I can't stay.'

He pulled over to the side of the road when he found somewhere he could stop. He pulled the lever he uses when he's stopped the car and turned round to face me properly, and put a hand gently on my knee.

'Don't be silly,' he said with a smile. 'I had a really, really fun time with you and everyone else. You have to go to your Mum's now, but you'll have fun there too, won't you?'

WHICH WAY IS NORTH?

I didn't answer the question. I had a million difficult thoughts that were hard to put into words. Of course I would have fun at my Mum's, but I wanted to stay at the cottage too. I didn't want to think my Dad was sad about having to take me away. I wanted to see my Dad more, and I knew that he wanted to see me as well, but I didn't understand why I couldn't just stay with him more. Everything just felt so big and *complicated*. I felt tears coming out of my eyes.

'Hey,' Daddy said. 'What's wrong?'

'I don't know,' I said.

'Are you crying?' he asked.

'No!' I turned my face away from him.

My Dad ticked my leg gently. 'It's okay. It's really okay.'

We sat for a little while talking about the fun things we had done that day, and I started to feel a little happier again. My Dad smiled talking about the ducks and the water, and all the fun games we played. I still felt a little sad that I had to leave early, but I liked that my Dad was trying to make me feel better.

'It *is* sad that we have to leave early,' Dad said. 'But we had a lot of fun while we were here, didn't we? And I'm sure you're going to have lots of fun at your Mum's. You're a lucky girl – you get to go to lots of places, see lots of people and do lots of things with your Mum *and* your Dad.'

'Yeah,' I said. And I even smiled a little bit.

'Did you like that ice cream earlier?' My Dad asked.

'Yeah,' I said again.

'Well, next time I've got you, why don't we go and get some more? Then it'll be like we're on holiday again.'

'Yeah,' I said, and I smiled even more.

'Great,' my Dad said. 'Let's get going then.'

He started the car and we drove down the long road. He reached back and patted my leg gently.

'I love you,' he said.

'I love you too.'

I must have fallen asleep not long after, and when I woke up I was at my Mum's house. I didn't feel very sad anymore, and I knew I would be feeling a little happier now, for a while at least.

WHICH WAY IS NORTH?

I hugged my Dad goodbye, and he kissed me on the head. I thought about Sophie shouting '*Ewww!*' at this again and I started laughing.

'Why are you laughing?' My Dad asked.

'Because I had a good time,' I said.

My mind rested for a little while.

CHRIS MORRIS

The Grave of David Wilson

I had no idea my run would spark an eerie mystery when I set out on Tuesday morning.

I set out for a small run around the observatory on what was a pleasant enough day and quite perfect for running; not too hot and not too cold. The observatory was situated at the side of a beautiful old cemetery, which dated all the way back to the seventeen-hundreds. As I ran, I distracted myself from the fatigue by reading some of the headstones, which were remarkably mixed in both age and style.

Brian Boyd
1923 – 1971
Beloved father of Michael
Rest in Peace

This was situated at the top of a small hill among a row of other headstones. Brian's was looking even older than

WHICH WAY IS NORTH?

some of the ones that predated it. It was brown and murky, moss covering many of the engraved letters and had no flowers at its foot.

Further on a beautiful headstone in the shape of a large, white angel read:

Hilary Smith
1960 – 2019
A heart of gold stopped beating,
Her time on Earth was fleeting,
Her life was short but her love was broad,
Rest now in heav'n, under thy God

The next few I noticed had eroded to such a point that I couldn't read the names, only the years.

M h e r
1820 – 1896

Fa y f H n
1798 – 1880

And then I came across one that stopped me in my tracks.

It was a large, beautiful gold and black headstone with fresh flowers laid all around it. There was a picture of more flowers scattered around the edges of the stone itself, and the engraved writing read:

In loving memory of David Wilson
1954 – 2020
Taken too soon from his partner Jean, daughter Amy, and son
Mike
Be at peace

I knew David. A little bit, anyway. His son Mike was a friend of mine. We had met at college and stayed friends long afterwards. His father had passed away quite suddenly, and it had been really hard for all the family. I attended the funeral, hugged Mike and his sister and mother afterwards. Mike had put on a brave face that day and had spoken some words about David. I admired him for it; he'd been close to his dad but remained composed during the eulogy while bringing many to tears.

WHICH WAY IS NORTH?

Mike and I hadn't spoken much since his father's passing back in February, mostly due to the virus that had then plagued the world and kept us all mostly indoors for months. I wondered how he was doing and decided that I'd send him a message when I got home.

I quickly showered after the run and got my phone out.

Hey Mike, how are you doing? How's this whole lockdown business treating you? I was just out for a run around Backhill Cemetery there, and I stumbled upon your dad's headstone. Beautiful tribute to him, had no idea it was there. Hope you're doing okay with it all.

Thinking nothing more of it, I started making myself some food. The run had made me quite hungry and more tired than usual, which was annoying considering how small a run it was. Did this mean I was getting less fit?

My phone buzzed. A message back from Mike.

Hey, thanks for the message. Yeah I'm doing fine, taking it a day at a time and that. Haha, I think you must have seen a ghost. My dad was cremated and his plaque is at the crematorium. Probably just another David Wilson. How are you doing?

A chill ran down my body. I read the message back again. *My dad was cremated and his plaque is at the crematorium. Probably just another David Wilson.*

But it *couldn't* be another David Wilson. Another David Wilson who died this year, had a wife called Jean and two children named Amy and Mike? I tried to assess the likelihood of it. Could it be possible? I supposed it could... But it was highly unlikely.

I typed a message back to Mike. *How old was your dad when he died?*

The reply came a minute later: *66, why?*

So, born in 1954?

Yeah. Why are you being weird?

At this point, I started to wonder if I'd possibly misread the whole thing. Was I going crazy? I decided to go back to the grave and see it again. That way, I could also make it clear to Mike that I hadn't muddled anything up.

When I arrived at the grave again, I read the whole thing three more times, very carefully.

WHICH WAY IS NORTH?

In loving memory of David Wilson
1954 – 2020
Taken too soon from his partner Jean, daughter Amy, and son
Mike
Be at peace

I stared in disbelief. Taking my phone out, I snapped a picture of it and sent it to Mike, who had viewed the message but didn't write anything back for the entire length of time it took me to walk back home. About an hour later, I got a message from him.

Is this a prank? Because if it is it's really not funny.

A prank? As if I'd do something like this! I felt a little bit insulted by Mike's message but then tried to put myself in his shoes. He'd just been sent an impossible image – his father's headstone in a cemetery, implying he was buried there. Beautiful flowers surrounding the grave, placed there by some unknown person or people. All the while, his father's remains had been burned, and a tribute was erected in the crematorium. This must have been blowing his mind!

I replied: *It's not a prank, I promise. Do you fancy a trip up there? You can see for yourself.*

Mike met me there that night, just before the sun began to set. We met at the gates and walked up towards the location of David's grave. The cemetery was quiet, and so were we as we walked through a thin air of foreboding. A light spitter of rain had begun to fall but the night was warm enough.

'It's just up here,' I said, and pointed towards the location of the headstone. As I did, I spotted a hooded figure standing at David's grave. Even just going by the person's pose, they looked sombre as they stood there. They were wearing a yellow raincoat and keeping a hand to the hood to stop it from blowing over.

'Mike...' I began, and stopped in my tracks. 'There's someone there.'

Mike looked up towards where I had pointed. 'Is that the grave? Where that person is?'

I nodded before Mike set off quickly towards the grave. 'Hey! You! Wait a minute!'

I didn't know if the figure had spotted Mike or if they had just come to the natural end of their visit, but they started to move away from the grave. I quickened my pace to catch up with Mike, who strode forwards with determination.

When we arrived at the grave, the person was gone. Mike stared at the headstone with a look of shock on his face. He leaned forwards and touched it softly, as though trying to learn something of where it had come from, and who had put it there.

'This is so weird,' Mike said, turning to look at me. 'This *must* be for him. But it also *can't* be.'

'I know,' I said. And I wished I had more to say, but the mystery had been puzzling me all day.

'I wish we'd caught whoever that was a minute ago.' Mike's face changed to a look one would have when arriving at a conclusion of some sort. 'I know what to do,' he said.

There was a small building that we hoped was some official premises for the cemetery. Arriving there we found that it was indeed a tiny office that was just closing for the night. The manager, a short middle-aged man with large glasses and a balding head, was the last to be leaving.

'I'm afraid I can't give out information like that,' the manager said. 'It's against data protection.'

'But that's my father's name on the stone,' Mike argued. 'David Wilson. I'm named on the stone too, Mike Wilson. Here, I can show you some ID.'

'You are *a* Mike Wilson, yes,' the manager agreed as he was pulling a shutter down over the main door. 'But we have on record the one person who is to be contacted in regards to Mr David Wilson's headstone and I'm afraid it's not you, so I can't discuss it with you. I'm sorry, I cannot tell you the name of the person who bought the place for Mr Wilson.'

The manager firmly but politely wished us a good night and walked away down the cemetery's path as the last light of the sun began to disappear. Mike turned once more to me.

'Well, there's only one thing for it,' he said. 'I'll have to dig up the grave.'

Alarmed, I placed a hand on my friend's shoulder. 'Don't be rash. Can you imagine the trouble you'd be in if you were caught? And what if you *did* find your dad there? What part of the mystery would be solved for you? I've got a better idea.'

The grave was undoubtedly looked after. Those flowers were fresh, and the grave obviously had at least one visitor now and then. I told Mike that since I lived really close to the cemetery, I would keep an eye out and watch for any more visitors. He seemed somewhat calmed by this, and I detected no more hint of a plan to go grave digging.

For the next few days, I made sure to either run or walk past David Wilson's grave. On the days I ran, I planned a route that would go past it two or three times and when I walked, I did so slowly, looking around for someone wearing a yellow raincoat as I went. Every time I saw the grave and the fresh flowers laid there, my mind tore itself to pieces trying to work out the solution to the mystery. By this point, I was convinced it was indeed Mike's father's grave, and so a million unresolved questions swam around inside my head.

This wasn't helped when I discovered a new object at the grave.

CHRIS MORRIS

I nearly hadn't noticed it at first. I would have walked past the headstone without looking back, and then perhaps would have never discovered this new piece of the ever-growing puzzle that was David's grave. Pausing in my step, I looked again towards the headstone and saw that I had indeed spotted what I thought I had; a small white envelope with the name *David* written in neat handwriting on the front.

I felt my heart leap in my chest. What could this mean? This envelope was addressed *to* David. Of course, he couldn't read it himself, so was it possible that whatever message contained inside was for someone else? Was it possible that someone had been watching me and wanted me to pick up the envelope and read the letter? And who left it here? The hooded figure? Or was this message intended *for* the hooded figure?

I had to find out, of course. I looked up and down the path and could see no other people, so I casually walked over to the grave. Crouching down and picking up the envelope, I stuffed it inside my jacket pocket and continued on my walk. I didn't want to risk reading the letter out in the open where anybody could spot me, so I

WHICH WAY IS NORTH?

kept it tucked away while I finished my walk and headed home.

When I got inside, I was shaking. I sat at my kitchen table and placed the envelope on it in front of me. The handwriting was indeed elegant, and looked as though it had been written with great care. As I turned the envelope around and prepared to tear the seal, I briefly wondered whether this was the right thing to do after all.

After a moment's internal debate, I ripped the envelope open.

Pulling out the single piece of paper within, I first noticed that the contents were written in the same beautiful handwriting. I read through the message slowly.

David Wilson,

You came to me so full of love,
It seemed gifted from the sky above,
you made me laugh, you made me cry,
It broke my heart to say goodbye.

CHRIS MORRIS

Here's to you, surreptitious man,
I never solved you, what woman can?
Here's to your life, your deeds and lies,
And whatever events from your death arise.

Go now, rest in peace,
On this grave make no mark or crease,
This grave be left or found by others,
It has stories to tell, Sisters and Brothers.

I read the poem through another few times, trying to work out whatever message may have been hidden in its verses. I had a few ideas, and there was only one person to discuss these with.

Needless to say, Mike was gobsmacked by the message. He stood in my kitchen forty-five minutes later, open-mouthed and trembling as he read the letter. His face had gone white.

'Whoever wrote this was sure your dad had some sort of secret,' I said.

WHICH WAY IS NORTH?

A secret he took to the grave, I thought, but decided that this would be insensitive to say out loud.

'Do you know of any secrets your dad kept?' I asked.

Mike shook his head. 'No. What kind of secret could he have had? This poem reads like it was some sort of dark thing. My dad having a dark secret? There's just no way; I mean, I know I'm biased and all, but he was a very good person. Never hurt a fly, helped others out where he could... he was full of love, you know?'

I nodded slowly. 'Any idea who could have written it?'

'Well, obviously a woman,' Mike said. 'But I have no idea. I don't recognise the handwriting. Not that I spend a lot of time examining other people's handwriting.'

'She seems convinced he lied about something,' I said. '"Here's to your life, your deeds and lies." I wonder what she means by that?'

'My dad wasn't a liar,' Mike said. But even as he spoke those words, I thought I could see the early seeds of doubt which had been sowed on his face.

Mike stayed for a while afterwards, and we tried to forget about the mystery temporarily.

I continued walking or running past David's grave, and the more I drifted past the now wilting flowers, the more I began to lose hope. Maybe this mystery was just never going to be solved; a bizarre secret which would sit there forever unexplained and endlessly haunting.

So I was somewhat relieved, but mostly nervous when finally I spotted that hooded figure I'd been searching for. On the day I saw the person again, I'd decided to sit on a bench and read my book. The first few minutes had gone by quickly, and I paid more attention to the grave than Agatha Christie, but when the book started to get really engaging I lost my focus on the grave and was swept away by *The Secret of Chimneys* instead.

When I glanced up from my book, I saw her. Yes, it was definitely a she. A woman who looked to be in her early sixties. This time the yellow raincoat was missing, but I knew it had to have been her. I closed my book and slowly approached the grave of David Wilson.

WHICH WAY IS NORTH?

The woman stayed fixed on the grave, and as I drew closer, I saw that she had genuine grief in her face. She didn't see me approach, so I spoke softly.

'Hi.'

She looked around and half-smiled. The rest of her face showed a shallow anxiety.

'Sorry,' she said. 'Do I know you?'

'I don't think so,' I said. 'But I think we may have known someone in common.' I indicated towards David's headstone.

'Ah,' she said. 'Yes. Maybe.'

'How did you know your David?' I asked.

'*My* David?' she chuckled. 'Yes, he was supposed to be mine. David and I were lovers, but he had his heart set on another woman.'

I probably couldn't hide the surprise and disgust in my face. And when I spoke, I would have made my feelings clear towards this woman. 'No! David? David was cheating on Jean?'

The woman drew a deep breath and sighed. 'I *am* Jean.'

CHRIS MORRIS

Utterly confused, I could only look at this woman standing in front of me in puzzlement.

'I know, I know,' she said. 'You must be confused. Let's sit down a while and talk.'

She sauntered towards the bench that I had previously been reading on. I sat with her there in the warmth of the afternoon sun.

'My name is Jean,' she said. 'The same as his other partner. The woman he married. I was with David for three years before I found out he had been seeing her. I was disgusted. Something about her having the same name as me made it worse. We split up, of course, and then he married Jean. The *other* Jean.'

'I can't believe it,' I said. 'David was always a friendly guy. Really funny. He's my friend's father.'

'Mike?' Jean asked. 'Or Amy?'

'Both, I suppose,' I said. 'But mostly Mike. I met him when we studied together.'

'From what I hear they're terrific kids,' Jean said. 'Well, they're not *kids* any more.'

'They were heartbroken when he died,' I said. 'Taken away too soon. Cancer. But you probably know

WHICH WAY IS NORTH?

that already. Mike said that when David was in hospital they gave him a crutch to help him walk and he picked it up and started pretending it was a flute. He was in high spirits until the very end.'

'Never smoked, never drank,' Jean said, and then scoffed. 'As far as I know, I suppose.'

'How do you know about them?' I asked. 'Mike and Amy, I mean?'

'Oh, life is funny,' Jean said. 'David and I splitting didn't mean the end for us. A few weeks after I found out about the cheating, I discovered I was pregnant.'

'Mike and Amy have another sibling?' I said with disbelief.

'They did,' Jean said. 'I miscarried.'

'Oh,' I said with sadness. 'Oh, I'm really sorry.'

'I had told David about the pregnancy,' Jean said. 'He decided he was going to be there for what was to be his first child. He said he was going to tell his girlfriend about me but was just working up the courage. I'm not sure he really ever was. He had lied so much up until this point. As the years went on, David and I continued to have mutual friend-of-friends, and I heard much about what was going on with him. I heard about his marriage, his children, and of course, his death.'

I paused a moment, trying to take all of this in. It seemed so unreal.

'So David's body...' I started.

'It was cremated,' Jean said. 'I bought the plot here for the headstone, but nothing was buried. I paid extra for it.'

'Why?' I asked.

Jean drew in another long breath before speaking. 'I was never able to fully let go of the pain that David had caused me. And for me to lose his baby but for him to go on to have this other life with other children... it stung me. I never looked Jean up to tell her about David and I. I didn't want the children to be hurt. But that pain never went away. When I heard of his passing, I thought about having the headstone made in the hopes that perhaps someone he knew would find it and discover his secret. That way, I didn't need to be too involved.'

'You could have just found Jean and told her,' I said.

WHICH WAY IS NORTH?

'Yes,' Jean agreed. 'But I rather thought I was past all the drama in my life.'

I didn't fully understand this. My head was swimming with what felt like a million thoughts.

'Are you going to tell Mike?' she asked.

I looked at her. I'd made my mind up about that. When I told her what I intended to do, she nodded in understanding.

Later that day, Mike called me. 'Have you found out anything about the headstone?' he asked.

CHRIS MORRIS

Second Chances Series 2 Episode 1: "The C Word"

Black screen.

Cue music - "Second Chances Theme – Slow Piano Version" by Maria Tomlin.

Voice of Janine Scott: 'Brian was lovely. Really lovely. We met at high school...'

Fade in artistically blurred, slow motion video of busy high school corridor. Pupils carrying books underarm while others push playfully at each other and laugh.

Janine Scott: 'We were never in any classes together, but he kept giving me the eye, you know? I was thrilled when he finally asked me out.'

Image changes to an equally blurry beach in the early evening. A couple walk hand-in-hand towards the ocean. A large, orange sun is half-hidden on the horizon and the first of the evening's stars begin to show.

WHICH WAY IS NORTH?

Janine Scott: 'He was a real charmer. He had a romantic side to him that none of his friends would ever have known about. We saw each other for about a year before he asked me to marry him.'

Image of a newlywed couple exiting a church. White confetti rains down on the happy pair as they walk down the stairs to applause from their guests.

Change of music - "Second Chances Theme – Happy Version" by Maria Tomlin.

Janine Scott: 'It was the perfect day, really. We were both delighted. My mum cried all day, and she kept saying sorry. She hugged Brian and kissed him on the cheek. That made him a wee bit uncomfortable, but he laughed it off. We had our first child the year after.'

Cut to hospital maternity ward scene. A proud, smiling new father holds his newborn baby, wrapped in a cosy blanket. The mother lies in bed, exhausted but overjoyed. The new family have their precious first embrace as one unit.

Janine Scott: 'She was bang on time, arrived on her due date. She barely cried. Three years later, we had our baby boy.'

Image switches to a happy family sitting on the floor. The mother and father laugh as a toddler places a block on top of a tower, and the tower collapses to the floor. The mother holds a beautiful newborn in her arms who watches with interest as the blocks slowly tumble to the floor.

Janine Scott: 'Everything was so perfect. We were all a happy family. I didn't think it would change.'

Music stops.

Image cuts to Janine Scott in the interview seat. A grey background is laid out behind her, and she looks off at the interviewer to her right. Her face is melancholy.

Voice of female interviewer: 'When did it start to go wrong?'

Janine Scott: 'Around Christma... Sorry, Christmas.'

'Shit, stop it there, stop! She stuttered.'

Phil, one of the editors, paused the video.

'Come on!' John groaned. 'This is the opener to the series. We didn't get the viewing numbers we were looking for last year, we need to get this perfect! We can't have stupid little mistakes like this. Can you edit the stutter out, Phil?'

'Gimme a sec,' Phil said, and he started clicking around the software before playing the video back.

Voice of female interviewer: 'When did it start to go wrong?'

WHICH WAY IS NORTH?

Janine Scott: 'Around – Christmas.'

'No, no,' John said. 'That doesn't work at all. You can see the image jump, and her voice goes weird. What if we just take out the "Around"?'

'We'll have to extend the family scene then,' Phil said. 'And then it'll just jump to Janine when she says "Christmas".'

'Did she pause for a bit after she said that?' John asked.

'I believe so, yeah,' Phil said. 'Stick another black screen on when Lisa asks when it started going wrong, then cut to Janine just as she speaks. Let's give it a try.'

Janine Scott: 'Everything was so perfect. We were all a happy family. I didn't think it would change.'

Music stops.

Black screen.

Voice of female interviewer: 'When did it start to go wrong?'

Image cuts to Janine Scott in the interview seat. A grey background is laid out behind her, and she looks off at the interviewer to her right. Her face is melancholy.

Janine Scott: 'Christmas.'

CHRIS MORRIS

Janine stares off into the distance before looking down at the floor.

Cue music - "Second Chances – Main Theme" by Maria Tomlin.

Cue title: "Second Chances". Subtitle: "The C Word".

'Great!' John enthused. 'Fantastic work, Phil. What an opener! That'll get the audience engaged for sure.

John had been asked to produce the second series of *Second Chances,* and he'd thought the title of the show to be quite peculiarly apt. He had just finished producing a flop of a show called *Tip Offs*. The premise of the show had been somewhat interesting; it was a look at the most unusual things that were found at rubbish tips around the country. The idea was to interview both the people who worked at the dump and also those who were getting rid of unusual items and track down the stories of how they had come to be discarded. John imagined that there would be a few interesting stories to tell. He had been wrong. He'd realised this on the first day of filming when an eccentric worker at one of the dumps had been interviewed.

WHICH WAY IS NORTH?

Yeah, we get a load of weird people coming in here with weird stuff, like. There was a guy once who came in with four big suitcases. I says to him, here you! What's in them suitcases? He opens one of them and inside was a load of newspaper! Unbelievable! Same day there was this young couple getting rid of a big load of unused carpet. Perfectly fresh stuff as well. I asked them why they weren't keeping it, they says they'd just moved into their new place, and they didn't need the trimmings. Then they just chucked it in! Can you believe that? Yeah, I've seen a lot of crazy stuff in my days here, like.

He never should have signed on to produce that one. The first season of *Second Chances* had come out around the same time, and it had done moderately well under a young producer who was new to the game. She'd moved on to another project and John had been asked by

Ryan, the show's creator, to step in. It had been made clear to him that the numbers last year needed to be improved on if the show was to be renewed. John didn't want to fail. This was both his and the show's own second chance.

'We got high numbers for the first episode in the last series,' Ryan had said. 'I'm not sure if you saw it? The one about the older guy who went back to school for a few months and sat the real exams?'

John had indeed seen the episode. It had been all over the news, and the man who had gone back to the schools had been funny, playing up to the cameras a bit but it had made for good television. John wasn't surprised that it had done so well.

'After that, the numbers dropped by quite a bit,' Ryan had said. 'Nobody was really interested in that woman's second chance at submitting a novel manuscript to the publishing company that had already passed on her, or the other guy's second chance at stand up comedy. God, he was awful. Not funny at all. Total cringe TV. Doesn't seem to work for our audience.'

'So what sort of thing do you think will work well?' John had asked.

A producer's second chance at producing a successful TV show? John had thought. *Jesus, you could make an episode from my own story.*

WHICH WAY IS NORTH?

Ryan had handed over a document then. Among the mass amount of data on the sheet, it contained a breakdown of the viewing numbers from each episode from season 1 of Second Chances. As Ryan had said, the "Back to School" episode was by far the most popular episode, but not very far from it was an episode called "Once a Cheater".

'Oh god,' John had said. 'What was that one about? Someone getting a second chance after being caught cheating on their partner?'

'You got it,' Ryan had said. 'You didn't see that one then? People love a juicy cheating story. You'll know yourself – it's in everything. There's hardly a TV show or movie or book that comes out now that doesn't involve cheating in some way. It draws people in, they're obsessed with that sort of story.'

'Ugh,' John had groaned. 'Yeah I know, it's awful. And it seeps into real life – life imitating art.'

'Or art imitating life?' Ryan had said.

'It's probably just a never-ending circle,' John had said.

'In any case,' Ryan had moved on. 'I need you to dig deep and find someone who's maybe willing to give their partner a second chance after they were cheated on. That will really draw in an audience, and we *need* an audience for this season. Otherwise, the whole series will be scrapped.'

John didn't like it, but he and his spent weeks researching and advertising to find six episodes of people receiving their second chances, and he particularly kept an eye out for cheaters. He didn't need to try very hard – alongside a substantial amount of older people wanting to go back to school, his inbox was filled with people from all around the country willing to appear on TV to give their other halves that second chance that they may or may not have deserved. John and his team spent hours upon hours reading through the emails and slowly whittling them down to just six, from which they planned to make episodes.

John was fairly confident but nervous. The series could potentially be excellent; they were going to follow a large fellow who had attempted a marathon last year but had had to pull out when he just couldn't continue. That would be a nice, emotional story, with hopefully a positive outcome for the guy. Then there was a woman who had previously tried to surprise her husband by redecorating the entire house while he had been away on a business trip, only when he had returned he had hated what she had done with the place. The house had remained in this state for the last two years, and now the show was giving the woman enough money to have a second chance at surprising her husband with a newly decorated house that was to everyone's taste.

A nice mix of emotional and funny stories. And then there was Brian and Janine's story. That was the one John was most anxious about.

'Right,' John said to Phil after they had finished editing the opening. 'What's the next thing that needs a look?'

Phil flicked through a notepad he had set at the side of his computer. 'I wanted you to take a look at the confession section.'

'Okay, roll it.'

Janine Scott in interview seat: 'So… I decided to confront him about it.'

CHRIS MORRIS

Black screen.

Cue text on screen:

"The following video was recorded on Janine's phone."

"It is being used with permission."

'Wait, wait,' John said. 'Why don't we add one more bit of text at the start, for a little more dramatic effect? Put "Janine decided to confront Brian about the letter" at the beginning. And take out "It is being used with permission", replace it with "Brian did not know he was being filmed". That'll be more engaging. Good, now let's continue.'

"Brian did not know he was being filmed."

Cue music - "Tension" by Maria Tomlin.

The camera wobbles as Janine places it in a position somewhere unseen. When she steps away, we see that we are in the family's kitchen. Brian steps into view moments after Janine walks away from the presumably obscured camera.

'Hi,' Brian says. He looks a little concerned. 'What's up? Is something wrong?'

'Take a seat,' Janine says. We can only see her back as she faces Brian. 'I want to talk to you about something.'

WHICH WAY IS NORTH?

'Okay...' Brian says, and the pair take a seat opposite each other at the kitchen table. 'What's wrong?'

'Do you have something you want to tell me?' Janine asks. Her voice shakes slightly.

'Like what?' Brian says. His eyes are fixed on Janine.

'Like anything?' Janine says. 'Something you should probably tell your wife?'

Brian stares at Janine, seemingly unable to speak.

There's a silence for a few seconds before Janine breaks it.

'I know, Brian,' She says.

'You know what?' Brian asks. He looks increasingly worried.

'I know about the letter,' Janine says, and she takes it out of her pocket before sliding it across the table to an aghast Brian, who looks down at it with an open mouth.

'Well?' Janine asks.

Brian begins to sob. 'I'm sorry, Janine. I'm so sorry.'

Cue music - "Drama" by Maria Tomlin.

Voice of interviewer over image of confrontation scene:

'Do you think Brian deserves a second chance?'

Cut to Janine in interview chair. She stares at the interviewer off-screen. She says nothing.

Fade to black.

'That's pretty good,' John said. 'I think we should take out the music during the confrontation though. It's a little too cheesy. Sometimes this stuff is more effective without the distraction of music. Then it'll be more effective when it comes in at the end when Brian apologises.'

Phil did as he was instructed, then played the scene back for John.

'Brilliant!' John said. 'Much better! That will really work. What's next?'

'I've got the interview with Brian,' Phil said. 'Still can't believe the guy agreed to be interviewed.'

'I know,' John agreed. 'Brave guy. Let's take a look.'

Image of the interview room where we've previously seen Janine. Brian takes a seat, and someone helps him attach the microphone to his shirt.

'Ugh, I hate it when I'm in these,' John said.

'Do you want me to take this bit out?' Phil asked.

WHICH WAY IS NORTH?

'No, no,' John said. 'My wife gets a good laugh out of it.'

Voice of the female interviewer: 'Why didn't you tell Janine?'

Brian heavily sighs. He looks uncomfortable. 'I don't know,' *he finally says.* 'I should have. I obviously should have, I just...'

Brian trails off. He seems stuck for words.

'Was it the children?' *the interviewer suggests.*

'Yes,' *Brian responds.* 'Partly, I suppose. I knew they would be hurt. I don't think they ever would have thought about their dad that way. I was... ashamed, I suppose.'

'Did you feel ashamed when your wife found the letter?' *the interviewer asks.*

Brian takes another deep breath and stares off into the distance. 'I never should have hidden it from her. It was stupid. Really stupid. I just never thought I was the type of person. The type of person to ch...'

'You know what?' John interrupted. 'I think this is all fine. We should take one more look at it after lunch, but I really want to make sure we've got the ending right. Can we have a look at that?'

CHRIS MORRIS

The footage that John and Phil had to work with was shot many months after the events that Brian had been describing in his interview. By this point, the *Second Chances* team had been in touch with both Brian and Janine, and had done some filming. If they could just edit this together in the right way, John thought they'd have a solid first episode for the new series. He was keen to take a look.

'Here we are,' Phil said. 'This is from... forty-nine minutes in.'

'Perfect,' John said. 'Let's see.'

Shot of a large, white building from the car park. The camera pans slowly upwards. It's a bright day, but the trees are bare. As the camera reaches the top, the sun glares in the lens.

Cue text on screen:

"Ten months later..."

'Get rid of that dot-dot-dot,' John said. 'It'll look better without it.'

"Ten months later."

'Okay,' John said. 'Now add some emotional music.'

Cue music - "Sad Piano Theme" by Maria Tomlin.

WHICH WAY IS NORTH?

Cut to the inside of what appears to be a waiting room. Brian sits with an anxious expression on his face. Next to him, Janine holds his hand and strokes it lovingly. She looks as though she's trying to put on a brave face.

'We should probably add that "filmed with permission" thing this time,' John said. 'The audience will need to be reassured.'

Cue text on screen:

"Filmed with permission from Albert Street Medical Centre."

Cut to another angle. From here we can still see Brian and Janine, but we can also see a large, electronic board. With a small beep, Brian's name flashes up on the board:

Brian Scott – Dr Baker
Room 05

Cut to Brian and Janine walking into Dr Baker's office. The camera wobbles slightly. On arriving, Dr Baker first greets the couple then makes eye contact with the camera.

'Damn,' John muttered. 'That doesn't look good. You know what, we don't really need the footage of them arriving at the office. We've already got the establishing shot of the centre anyway. Just go straight to them sitting at the doctor's desk after the shot of the board. And cut the music there too.'

Music cuts.

Shot of Brian and Janine sitting anxiously at Dr Baker's desk. Dr Baker pulls a folder out of a filing cabinet and sits opposite them.

'Okay,' the doctor says. 'Well Brian, I have the results here. As you know, the chances of your cancer clearing were about fifty-fifty. I know that's not the most reassuring thing to hear, but...'

Cut to Brian, looking as anxious as ever.

Dr Baker continues. 'I have some good news.'

Cut to Dr Baker, who is now smiling.

'You're in remission.'

Cut to Janine, who gasps and places a hand over her mouth. Tears can be seen in her eyes.

Cut to Brian, who just looks shocked.

Cut back to Dr Baker, who is still smiling. 'You'll need to keep having some tests for a while,' he says. 'But I can tell you, things are looking promising for an all-clear.'

WHICH WAY IS NORTH?

'Stop,' John said, and Phil paused the video. 'Here's where we should put in our royalty music. What have we got to work with?'

Phil opened a folder on the computer and scrolled through. 'Let's see,' he said. 'We've got Snow Patrol, Chasing Cars?'

'Ugh,' John muttered. 'Overused. It's in everything now, isn't it? What else?'

'Everybody Hurts, REM… That old Sia song that's used all the time now… Oh, what about Fix You by Coldplay? Instrumental version. We haven't used that for a while.'

'I suppose,' John thought. 'You know what, yeah, stick that in. It's been a while since it was used for every sob story on X-Factor. Let's see how that works.'

Cue music - "Fix You – Instrumental Version" by Coldplay.

Mixed shots of Brian and Janine embracing and sobbing happy tears, Dr Baker looking on with a smile, the pair exiting the medical centre holding hands and laughing, returning home and hugging their children.

CHRIS MORRIS

Voice of female interviewer overlapping these scenes: 'How do you feel to be cancer-free?'

Cut to Brian and Janine sitting in the interview room together.

Brian - 'I'm so happy. So happy. It's like I've been given another chance, you know? A second chance at life. I feel really grateful.'

Interviewer: 'Do you think Brian deserves a second chance?'

Janine stares off-camera for a moment before replying: 'Of course he does. Nobody more so than him.'

Janine looks at Brian with a smile. They hold hands and Brian gives Janine's a gentle squeeze.

Cue text, which fades onto a black screen just as the music strikes its last chord:

"Second Chances"

'Stop,' John said. 'That's it. We've got it. It's perfect.'

WHICH WAY IS NORTH?

Second Chances Series 1 Episode 2: "Back to School"

Halley's comet passes the Earth and is visible to the naked eye only once every seventy-five to seventy-six years. This gives the average person just once chance to see it, but some are granted an extra opportunity: a second chance.

On the nineteenth of May 1910, Halley's Comet passed especially close to Earth, giving the people at the time an extraordinary view for six majestic hours.

Margaret Kelly was five years old when the comet passed. Her mother and father had been astronomers and were very excited about this once in a lifetime event. Their enthusiasm was so palpable that little Margaret became excited about seeing the comet to the point that she couldn't think of anything else.

Unfortunately, Margaret became very ill with flu and spent most of the time sleeping or using the bathroom. She missed the comet altogether.

However, on the eighth of March 1986, Margaret Kelly was afforded her *second chance*.

She was ill again, but she was wrapped up in a warm blanket, sat on the porch of her little house with a hot cup of tea, and she had the perfect view of Halley's Comet as it zoomed over her head. It wasn't as spectacular as the one she missed in 1910, but Margaret was thrilled nonetheless. She had waited an entire lifetime for this moment, and now she had finally made it up to herself. She had seen Halley's Comet.

Margaret passed away the very next day. But the second chance she was awarded had meant that she had left this world fulfilled, and had given some comfort to her family.

Being given a second chance is an extraordinarily valuable thing. For some of us, we receive many chances. For others, not even a single chance. *Second Chances*, beginning on television next year, will explore a wide range of everyday people being granted their very own second chance. It was created in memory of Margaret by her grandson, Ryan Kelly. If you think you should be awarded a second chance at something, apply to be on

WHICH WAY IS NORTH?

the show today. Don't miss out, you may not get another chance!

***

'What subject do you think you'll do the best at?'

The interviewer asked Joe this question with a bright smile. She had introduced herself as Jenny, and Joe thought she was very friendly. He had sat down on the interview chair and was answering questions as cheerfully as a dog in a sausage factory when this one had particularly enthused him.

'Oh, Geography,' he said with a slight scoff as though everyone should have already known that he was a Geography master. 'I know all the capital cities in every country in the world. Go on, name one.'

'Oh,' Jenny said, startled. 'I don't think we can…'
'It's okay,' Louise, the producer of the show, said to Jenny's side. 'Just go with it.'

'Okay,' Jenny said. 'Um… Argentina.'

'Buenos Aries,' Joe answered instantly. 'Easy. Gimmie a hard one.'

'Umm,' Jenny thought. 'Afghanistan?'

'Kabul!' Joe said with a grin. 'Come on! I said hard!'

'Right, okay... Err, Mongolia?'

'Ooohh,' Joe mused. 'Good one, good one. See, a lot of people would stumble on that one. Loads of people wouldn't have a clue. But see me? I'm a Geography *whizz*. The capital of Mongolia is Ulaanbaatar. That's Ulaan, U, L, double-A, N, Baatar, B double-A, T, A, R. Population of one-point-three million people. I tell you, I'll probably be asked to *teach* the geography class. I love it.'

'Alright,' Louise said. 'Thanks Joe, let's wrap it up there. See you tomorrow for your first day back at school!'

Joe Fraser had applied to appear on the television show *Second Chances*. He had read an article a few months ago about the programme and decided it might be an idea to have a second go at school. He'd failed most of his exams as a child but decided he'd matured much in the years later, and now at the age of fifty-six, he was sure he could go back and ace his exams.

WHICH WAY IS NORTH?

Four months of being back in a proper school, among the proper pupils, as long as the TV crew were allowed to film. The best thing was, the Scottish Qualifications Authority had even agreed that Joe could sit the real exams at the end, and gain real qualifications. It was an unprecedented move, but many thought that the organisation were trying to get back in the public's good books after the exam results debacle of 2020.

He would be taking five classes; Maths and English were a must, but Joe was allowed to freely choose the other three. Geography was top of his list, and he also enthusiastically picked Music. Then he was torn between Biology and Physics, before deciding that he wasn't actually all that interested in science anyway and went with French.

The producer, Louise, had eagerly tried to persuade him to choose PE, thinking the scenes of him trying to keep up with the kids would make for excellent television, but Joe explained rationally that a man in his mid-fifties would have little need for a new qualification in sport (but that if he'd done this ten years ago, he'd have effortlessly wiped the floor with the other students).

CHRIS MORRIS

So his five subjects chosen, Joe walked back into school with determination and glee.

Subject 1: English.

Joe was a well-read sort of individual. He'd managed in his fifty-six years of life to accumulate a library of read material which was larger perhaps than the combined total of his classmates. The problem was, most of what Joe liked to read was true crime.

'The thing is,' Joe had explained to the class on his first day. 'You *can* smuggle things into jail, but they usually do it up the...'

'All right!' Miss Johnson had interrupted, but there was no point. The kids in the class were already howling with laughter. 'Joe Fraser, will you keep your stories to yourself, please.'

'Sorry miss,' Joe had said deliberately sheepishly. They'd gone on to discuss tautograms. To Joe's pleasure, most of the class didn't know what they were, so he stood up and confidently recited one.

WHICH WAY IS NORTH?

'Tautograms truly transcend terrible travesties triumphantly.'

The class had a fit of giggles again.

'Mister Fraser, please sit down,' the teacher demanded.

'Wibble wobble washboard waywords, whitened wary walking wet. I made that one up just there.'

'Sit down, Joe!!' Miss Johnson yelled.

Joe tutted. 'All right!' Then as he sat down with a wry smile at the giggling classmates, playfully added: 'Sufferin' succotash.'

The room erupted into laughter once more.

'All right, Joe!' Miss Johnson yelled again. 'Punishment exercise! Twenty lines copied out and handed to me first thing tomorrow, please. "Punishments predict pandemonium, preferably predetermined!"'

'Very good miss!' Joe enthused. 'Did you make that up on the spot?'

Subject 2: French.

'It's just fancy English, isn't it?' Joe quipped.

Monsieur Bell, the French teacher, gave Joe an irritated look. 'No.'

'Ah, don't you mean *non*, Monsieur?' Joe's classmates chuckled at this. 'What's French for television again?'

'Never mind, Joe,' Monsieur Bell said.

'No, no,' Joe grinned. 'Honestly, what is it again? I forgot.'

Monsieur Bell sighed and rolled his eyes. '*Télévision.*'

The class, to Joe's delight, lit up in laughter.

'That's enough!' Monsieur Bell demanded.

'Oh no,' Joe said softly to the pupil sitting next to him, a young boy of sixteen who looked somewhere in between enjoying the hilarity of having Joe in his class and feeling a little awkward about it. 'That'll be my next punishment exercise. Fifty lines in French - "I will *non* make *le funny jokes* in Mister Bell's class any more."'

'It's *Monsieur*,' Monsieur Bell, who had obviously overheard Joe said.

'Why?' Joe asked.

'Excuse me?' Monsieur Bell said.

WHICH WAY IS NORTH?

'Why's it *Monsieur?*' Joe pronounced the last word in an over the top French accent.

'Because this is French class,' Monsieur Bell said mater-of-factly.

'But the other teacher just gets called *Mister*,' Joe pointed out. 'Are you actually French? Where are you from?'

'Paisley,' Monsieur Bell said.

'Oh!' Joe said with expressed interest. 'Do they speak French in Paisley?'

Monsieur Bell chose to ignore this. 'Alright now settle down everyone. Listen to the next example and write down your answer.'

Joe looked at the multiple-choice question on the paper in front of him.

Listen to the following excerpt and identify which sport Pierre likes to play.

A: Rugby
B: Football
C: Cricket

CHRIS MORRIS

D: Basketball

Monsieur Bell played the audio file on his computer.

'Bonjour! Je m'appelle Pierre. J'aime les cours de gym à l'école. J'aime faire du sport...

J'aime le football.'

Joe stifled his laughter before asking the teacher if he could hear it again because he wasn't sure whether it was cricket or rugby.

'Next question,' Monsieur Bell said, ignoring Joe. Joe read the question.

Listen to the following excerpt and identify which school subject Arielle enjoys.

A: Maths
B: Science
C: History
D: Music

Monsieur Bell played the next file.

WHICH WAY IS NORTH?

'Salut! Je m'appelle Arielle. J'aime aller à l'école. Mon sujet préféré est la musique. J'adore la musique.'

'Musique…' Joe mumbled. 'Musique… What's that again, maths?'

Monsieur Bell made Joe stand outside the classroom for the rest of the lesson.

Subject 3: Geography

'Did you know there's only one US state that begins with A and doesn't end with A?' Joe enthusiastically asked Mrs Smith, the Geography teacher.

'Yes, it's…' she began.

'Arkansas!' Joe interrupted. 'And I know what you're thinking too, you're thinking it ends with a W.'

'No,' Mrs Smith started.

'It doesn't!' Joe said. 'It ends with an S! S for silly, like whoever named the place, eh?'

'Well, regardless…' Mrs Smith tried to continue.

'But that's the easy bit of Geography,' Joe said. 'I can name you any capital city from any country in the world. It's all up here, you know, in my head. Go on, test me!'

Mrs Smith stalled for a moment before giving off a look of determination. A look which suggested she knew she probably shouldn't engage with this, but that she wanted to, and she wanted to win.

'Sudan?' Mrs Smith asked.

'Khartoum,' Joe replied confidently. 'And Juba is the capital of South Sudan, which gained independence from the Republic of Sudan in 2011, making it the newest country in the world.'

Mrs Smith looked slightly irritated by Joe's confident (and correct) response. 'Swaziland?'

'Swaziland?' Joe asked with a confused look. 'Oh! Mrs Smith, you mean Eswatini? You know it changed its name in 2018, don't you? You'll need to update your maps. Anyway, its capital is Mbabane. Well, that's its executive capital anyway. Its legislative capital is Lobamba. Funny thing is, neither of those cities is even the biggest. The largest one is Manzini, population of over one hundred thousand.'

WHICH WAY IS NORTH?

The pupils of Mrs Smith's Geography class looked both impressed and humoured as Joe spoke. Mrs Smith, in an apparent attempt to not be embarrassed, asked one more.

'Excellent, Joe. Top of the class for capital cities. Last one. What's the capital of Guam?'

Joe looked puzzled. He scratched his head. 'Guam? That's an... island, isn't it?'

'Yep,' Mrs Smith said with a smug grin on her face and her arms neatly folded.

'Islands can't have *capitals,* can they?'

'Some do. Guam is one of them,' Mrs Smith said.

'Well,' Joe sighed. 'You've stumped me on this one, sorry. You win, I suppose.'

Mrs Smith smiled in victory. She opened her mouth to speak.

Joe interrupted her before she could make a sound.

'Only kidding, it's Hagåtña. There's a little circle above the first A and a wavy line above the N. It's only a village, but it's the official capital.'

The class laughed once more as Mrs Smith's smile disappeared.

'Population of about a thousand I think.' Joe said with his signature grin.

'There's more to Geography than capital cities,' was Mrs Smith's only reply.

Subject 4: Maths

'What!?' Joe exclaimed. 'You get to use a *calculator* in the exam!?'

'You'll have two papers,' Mr Bale repeated. 'A calculator and a non-calculator one.'

Joe's mouth hung open in disbelief before his face turned into a disbelieving smirk. 'Nah, you're pulling my leg, aren't you? Wouldn't have happened in my days at school. We did all our thinking in our heads.'

'Yes, I remember,' Mr Bale said. 'I would have gone to school around the same time as you, Joe. But times have changed, and there's now a paper in which you're allowed a calculator. But you obviously have to know what to do with it.'

WHICH WAY IS NORTH?

'Woah, woah, woah!' Joe sounded. 'You would have gone to school about the same time as me? You don't look the same age as me. You're in your forties, surely?'

'Well, that's flattering Joe, but sadly no.'

'*Fifties* then?' Joe asked, aghast.

'Yes, fifties Joe, now, trigonometry...'

'Fifty what?' Joe asked.

'Fifty-six,' Mr Bale answered, apparently trying to just move on.

'Fifty-six!' Joe exclaimed. 'Same as me! What school did you go to?'

'Hillside Academy,' Mr Bale said.

'That was my school!'

Joe's classmates were interested in this. 'Do you two not know each other then?' one of them asked.

'Bale...' Joe mused. 'Was there a Bale in my class?'

Mr Bale eyed Joe, and a sudden look of realisation came upon his face.

'Richard!' Joe said excitedly. 'Your name's Richard Bale! We used to call you Ritchie! Can't believe I didn't recognise you! Ritchie! How are you doing!?'

Mr Bale's face had gone slightly scarlet.

'Remember that time you asked that girl out in class?' Joe asked. 'What was her name? Amy! What a time you picked, right in front of everyone else. And we all laughed at you when she said no!'

Joe's classmates enjoyed this thoroughly.

Hahahaha!!

Mr Bale got rejected!

Right in the middle of a class!

'It wasn't the worst thing though, was it?' Joe said. 'There was Lisa as well. She slapped you in the face in the middle of assembly because she saw you kissing Mary.'

Mr Bale had to exit the classroom for a few moments to regain his composure, during which time Joe enthusiastically told his classmates more.

Subject 5: Music

'Put the guitar down, Joe!' Mr Laidlaw instructed. Joe apologised and did as he was told. He had just been showing off the chords he knew on guitar and treated the class a rendition of a self-composed song:

WHICH WAY IS NORTH?

'Well I love my music and I love my songs,
I love this gee-tar and I ain't wrong,
But the one thing I can't have enough of,
No matter how much luck,
Is a kiss from my woman and a really good…'

This was where Mr Laidlaw had stopped Joe.

'If you had let me finish,' Joe said. 'You would have discovered a hidden love of mine. Monster trucks.'

Mr Laidlaw moved the lesson on, despite the uproar from the class.

'Now,' he said when the class had settled down. 'Who can tell me what *accelerando* means?'

'That sounds Italian,' Joe said, puzzled.

'Yes, it is,' Mr Laidlaw confirmed.

'Oh,' Joe said, surprised. 'Sorry, I must be in the wrong class. I thought this was music.'

'It is,' Mr Laidlaw said. 'Sit down, Joe.'

'What do we need to know Italian for?' Joe asked.

'It's a musical term,' Mr Laidlaw said.

'Why's it in Italian?' Joe enquired.

'Because a lot of musical terms come from Italian,' Mr Laidlaw said. 'You'll find them in musical notation everywhere. It used to be very difficult for the publishers to have to translate all of them into different languages.'

'Used to?' said Joe. 'But we can now, can't we? Why don't they just put it in English for us now?'

'Well, because...' Mr Laidlaw started. He looked slightly confused. 'Because they just don't. It's part of the exam, you'll have to know all of this. Now, what does *accelerando* mean?'

'I don't know,' Joe answered. 'But I think I know somebody who will know.'

'Who's that?' Mr Laidlaw asked.

'Miss Johnson,' Joe said. 'My English teacher.'

'Why?' Mr Laidlaw asked.

'She's an English teacher,' Joe said. 'She must have read that *Harry Potter* book. Sounds like one of his spells.'

***

'Who would like to go first?'

Jenny looked around at the five teachers. They all looked stressed, and no wonder too: not only had they all had to endure several weeks of Joe in their classes, but of course they had all been preparing the regular students for their exams too, which were now taking place.

'What about you, Mr Bale?' Jenny suggested.

Mr Bale sighed. 'Okay. I had my last lesson with Joe in the class last week, and I wrote his report not long afterwards.' He produced a sheet of paper which he now read from. 'I gave him ten out of ten for attendance, but sadly I had to score him low for his behaviour in class.'

'Why was that?' Jenny asked.

'Well...' Mr Bale started. 'His behaviour was often... erm... inappropriate.'

'Inappropriate in what way?' Jenny asked.

'Was it the stories he told about you in your high school days?' Miss Johnson asked with a slight smirk on her face.

Mr Bale spun round in his chair. 'How do you know about that!?'

'Word gets around,' Miss Johnson said. 'Brian McDermott from your class is in my English class. He told me about what Joe said, about that time in high school that you started crying when your history teacher yelled at you.'

'I was *not* crying!' Mr Bale protested. 'I get tears in my eyes when I yawn! It happens to a lot of people!'

'Wait,' Mrs Smith interrupted. 'I heard something like that too, from another pupil. He said that Joe said that someone in your class at the time said that you cried in your English class when you got to the end of *Charlotte's Web*.'

'*Charlotte's Web?*' Miss Johnson said. 'In high school?'

'It's okay Richard,' Mr Laidlaw comforted. 'I cried at the end of that one too.'

'I didn't cry!' Mr Bale exclaimed.

'Okay, okay,' Jenny said, raiding a hand. 'Let's just try to continue. 'Monsieur Bell? You've been pretty quiet. Would you like to give us your report of Joe?'

Monsieur Bell calmly cleared his throat and spoke. 'Joe était le clown de la classe...'

'Oh,' Jenny interrupted. 'Sorry, can you give it to us in English?'

'He said Joe was the class clown,' Mr Laidlaw said. 'I speak a little French.'

WHICH WAY IS NORTH?

'Well, that was easy anyway,' Miss Johnson said. '*Clown de la classe*....It just sounds like English, only fancier.'

Monsieur Bell looked wildly irritated. 'Je ne donnerai mon rapport qu'en Français.'

'Sorry?' Jenny asked.

'He said he will give his report...' Mr Laidlaw started.

'Only in *Français*,' Miss Johnson finished. 'Which probably means "French".'

'Let me see,' Mr Laidlaw held a hand out to Monsieur Bell, who handed him the report card. After a quick scan of the report, Mr Laidlaw nodded his head. 'Yes, it's written all in French.'

'Why's that?' Jenny asked Monsieur Bell.

'Parce que de cette façon, Joe pourrait enfin mettre un peu d'effort,' Monsieur Bell said.

'It's to make him finally put in some effort,' Mr Laidlaw roughly translated.

'How would you rate Joe's behaviour in class?' Jenny asked Monsieur Bell.

'Merde,' Monsieur Bell said.

Jenny looked to Mr Laidlaw, who said that he wasn't sure he should repeat in English what Monsieur Bell's response was.

Jenny turned now to Joe's Geography teacher. 'Mrs Smith, were you at all worried that Joe knew more capital cities than you did?'

'Oh come on,' Mrs Smith said. 'You saw me test *him* on capital cities, but you never saw me get tested. I know just as much as he does. Goes without saying, I'm a Geography teacher for goodness sake.'

'Great,' Jenny said, and she produced a sheet of paper from her clipboard.

'What's that?' Mrs Smith asked. She looked worried all of a sudden.

'We thought it might be fun for the show to give you a little test,' Jenny said. 'Just five questions. Are you ready?'

Mrs Smith had gone pale, but she answered with a strong voice. 'Yes. Yes, go ahead.'

'Alright,' Jenny said. 'What's the capital of Cambodia?'

WHICH WAY IS NORTH?

Mrs Smith relaxed a little. 'Phnom Penh. Wonder if Joe knows that one.'

'Good,' Jenny said. 'South Korea?'

'Seoul,' Mrs Smith replied, and there was a small smile forming on her face now.

'Great,' Jenny said. 'What about Sierra Leone?'

'*Sierra Leone?*' Mrs Smith asked, disbelievingly. 'Oh, come on. I didn't give Joe a hard one like that! He wouldn't know that one!'

'We gave him the same test earlier today,' Jenny said. 'He scored five out of five. He even gave the populations of each city.'

'This is just silly,' Mrs Smith said. 'What's this got to do with Joe, anyway? Do you want my report?'

'What's wrong?' Mr Bale asked with a small chuckle. 'You scared Joe's going to get your job?'

Mrs Smith turned to Mr Bale with a look of fury. 'You're just glad the spotlight's off of you! You know, Joe told me that you wet yourself in class once?'

'What!?' Mr Bale exclaimed.

'Yes,' Mrs Smith continued. 'In Maths.'

'I spilled water on myself!' Mr Bale explained.

The five teachers started squabbling among themselves while Jenny tried to calm the situation down. When they were quiet, Jenny managed to get them each to give their prediction for Joe's final grade.

'B,' Miss Johnson said.

'D,' Mrs Smith said.

'C,' Mr Laidlaw said.

'I don't have a clue,' Mr Bale said.

'Échouer,' Monsieur Bell said.

Jenny looked once again to Mr Laidlaw for a translation, who just looked confused.

'I think he said "pig",' Mr Laidlaw said.

Monsieur Bell placed his head in his hands and mumbled: 'sacré bleu.'

***

In terms of success, the second episode of the first series of *Second Chances* was the most popular. But for Joe, he received a mixed bag of exam results. He surprised himself when he found that his best result was for maths, much to the despair of Mr Bale, who had been interviewed on the show and had indicated how upset he was about Joe's mockery of him in front of his students.

WHICH WAY IS NORTH?

He had pretty good results for music and English too, although he did write "Ask JK Rowling" for his answer to one of the music questions. The examiner would no doubt get a laugh out of that, Joe had thought.

He scraped a pass in French. For every answer he wasn't sure of he just wrote the English word and either added some accents or the occasional "eu" or "aux" at the end (such as "schooleu" or "pencilaux"). As it happened, he got around 30% of these guesses correct.

Unfortunately, he failed Geography. Capital cities, as it turned out, weren't part of the exam.

CHRIS MORRIS

Is There Anybody Out There?

I don't like it here, Chris thought. Everything is so bleak. Where is the colour? Where are the sounds?

A slow scan of the environment filled Chris with a sort of despair. This place was like nowhere he had ever been. And yet it was full of memories. *His* memories. Memories that should be happy, so why do they hurt so much?

It looked sort of like a field, only grey. There were abandoned farm vehicles scattered around the landscape. When Chris looked at them, he somehow knew that none of them had been used in an incredibly, inconceivably long time.

'Hello!?' he yelled. 'Is there anybody out there!?'

His voice echoed around the chill, grey fields, and the wind carried it back to him. He suddenly realised he was a little underdressed for this place, wearing nothing but a pair of shorts and a t-shirt. The wind whispered

WHICH WAY IS NORTH?

around his arms and legs, and his skin crawled with goosebumps.

'*Hello!?*'

He was getting desperate. Surely, there must be *someone* here?

But there's not. There's nobody here because you deserve to have nobody. Everybody has left you, and everybody was right to. Your family hate you, your girlfriend left because she couldn't stand you, as soon as your daughter is old enough then she'll leave you too. You have no friends because you are simply insufferable. Who would want to hang out with a loser like you? You seem like a fun guy from the outside; funny, talented, kind and caring. But when people get to know you, when they get to know the **real** *you that is, what do they find? A pathetic, ambition-less, stupid, useless man. No wonder nobody wants to speak to you. No wonder you are alone.*

The tears that fell down Chris' cheeks didn't help. What was it Charles Dickens said? *Heaven knows we need never be ashamed of our tears, for they are the blinding dust upon the earth, overlying our hard hearts.* Something like that. But Chris felt immense shame in these tears. For every tear that dropped, proof was shown of his utter worthlessness.

Yes, look at the tears. Other people would rise up in his situation and do something about their lives. Not him. Not Chris. He's been defeated.

'HELLOOO!!??'

He fell to his knees beside a dull tree with no leaves. He grasped at its branches and wept, staring ashamedly at the ground beneath him. He imagined this world shrinking and bending around him, swallowing him up forever. The thought might have been slightly comforting if it weren't for the fact he knew it wouldn't happen.

'How did it come to this?' Chris whispered. 'How did I end up here? Everything's so wrong. So wrong. Where did I go wrong?'

He closed his eyes, but it was painful. As soon as his eyelids closed, he saw faces. Faces of people he loved, but they were sad. He saw his girlfrie… He saw his ex-girlfriend. Tears streamed down her face, and she looked at him with anger.

WHICH WAY IS NORTH?

'Why did you have to go and mess it up, Chris? Why? We could have had something good, but instead you come into my life and make it worse? What did I do to you to deserve that? I thought you loved me? Yet I was never good enough for you, was I? Everything questioned all the time. Well I'm sorry, okay? I'm sorry! I'm sorry I'm not absolutely perfect, I'm sorry I have bad days where I can't shift my mood, and I'm sorry that you *had* to put up with all of that. Poor Chris. Poor, self-centred, ungrateful Chris. We're over. Don't ever speak to me again.'

Chris wanted to say something back to her, but she disappeared. Her face was replaced by the young, five-year-old face of his own daughter.

'Daddy, do I *have* to come to your house? I want to stay at my Mummy's house. Your house is *boring.* You're boring. You just look sad all the time. You sound sad all the time. And I have nobody else to play with. Where's your girlfriend gone? I liked her. I don't want to come to your house for Christmas, I was to stay at my Mummy's. Please don't make me come to you any more.'

He tried to speak to her, but all he could manage were bursts of more tears. His daughter held a look of sheer disappointment in her beautiful little face. The kind of look that someone shouldn't know until later years.

'Why are you crying, Daddy? Can't you handle it?'

She disappeared.

Chris stood up and ran. He ran across the grey fields and he saw nothing else that would bring even the faintest spark of joy. The cold wind rattled around the bare trees and abandoned tractors.

'What is this place!?' Chris cried as he ran. 'Where am I? How do I get out!?'

He was running uphill, weeping as he went. He could smell something now – a faint but obvious smell of fire. As the top of the hill approached, he began to see a cloud of thick, black smoke. When he reached the top, he saw a building far in the distance. He recognised his workplace instantly, even though it was so far away. And outside it were all of the people he worked with. The building was on fire, and the people around it stood with their arms folded, staring at Chris with livid expressions.

WHICH WAY IS NORTH?

'This is your fault!' they cried. 'You did this! You gave us hope and then you took it all away! Why? Why, Chris!?'

Chris sank to his knees once more. He felt heavier suddenly, as though something had begun to push on him from the shoulders. Even now he could see his knees sink into the ground. He watched as first his legs, and then his stomach began to disappear into the ground below. The faces of his ex-girlfriend and daughter joined the others at the burning building as his head finally sank below the ground.

***

It's inescapable, this feeling. It draws you in like poisoned air into fractured lungs, and when it gets hold of you, it never lets go. It lets you think that you've come to the end; the end of everything joyful and bright and good in this world. Your very existence feels trapped in this preordained prison that was built with the understanding that one day you would be confined here to rot away the rest of your meaningless years. It's getting dark now, but what's the difference? There's no real light in this place anyway, and even if there was, all it would do is shine a sordid light on all of your transgressions in life, and who wants to see that? Who wants to see a pitiful venture into a life not worth batting an eyelid at? Who have you ever developed such a bond with as to show them your life laid out bare, nothing hidden, the real *you* exposed in all of its dirty lowliness? Who could you ever feel comfortable enough with to let them see this, and feel little or no shame? Who could ever love that? This is it now. You may as well get used to it. Imagine yourself a place where it never stops raining. A place so cold and miserable that even the dark creatures of the night avoid it. This is a place for people of unimaginably low measure. You fear people like this, but deep inside you know you're one of them. Not just *one* of them either – you are a prime example of this sort of person. Inside this horrid place is a dark hut which you call home, and inside this hut is nothing. Even when you bring something inside – a slice of bread, a box, a piece of thread – it disappears, and you don't even have the decency to feel sad about it any more. Things that used to have the potential to make you happy fade away and you no longer even care because once you were a man of ambition, but now you have resigned yourself to what you call your "fate" or "destiny", which is to remain hidden from the eyes of the people above you (of which there are plenty) for fear of being judged for exactly what you are: a complete failure. You even know that there used to be others here; people who you have admired and respected in the past, those who have found themselves weighed down by seemingly insurmountable forces and have had the courage to break free of their shackles and move onwards to find better places. You don't have their courage, as much as you pretend that you do. They have had the wherewithal to consider other paths while you have been rightly left behind in their dust to feed off misery and destitution. You might as well board up the windows and the door to your pathetic little hut and stop bothering other people with your petty matters of significant insignificance. And every time you *think* you see a light (or create one for yourself out of imaginary dust) just stop. Don't bother with hope because you've drained the life out of it and there's nothing left there for you. Better now to accept who you are and just stop making things worse. Not that they can get much worse of course, because you've hit it. Yes, it's as clear as a fresh spring day that you've hit your *rock bottom*. And even that is pathetic – the fact that your lowest point is someone else's every day. You can't handle it. Imagine swapping shoes with someone who has *real* problems, your suffering then would be inconceivable because you just don't have the mantle for it. Go now, close your eyes and let it all envelope you as you knew it one day would. The fight is over. It was over a long time ago, and you should have just welcomed it then; at least by now you'd be used to it, and it may have become easier.

Does it though? Do these things become easier? Is that even possible?

There's only one way to find out…

***

'Chris? Chris? Can you hear me?'

Chris sprung awake. He didn't know where he was now. Somewhere completely dark. It would have been bleak if it weren't for the relief of just seeing nothing at all.

'Who's there?' Chris asked.

WHICH WAY IS NORTH?

'It doesn't matter who I am,' the voice said. 'You just need to listen.'

'Go away,' Chris moaned, and he closed his eyes.

'Snap out of this!' the voice demanded. 'Snap out of it right now! You have to go back out there.'

'*What!?*' Chris spat. 'You can't be serious! It's done! There's nothing out there for me now. Everything's all messed up. I can't do it.'

'Can't...' the voice started. 'Or won't?'

'*I can't!*' Chris insisted.

'Oh. Well. Fair enough then,' the voice said. 'You just going to stay here then?'

Chris considered it. 'I would if I could.'

'No you wouldn't,' the voice argued.

'Yeah?' Chris questioned. 'What do you know?'

'I know that you feel like giving up,' the voice said.

'Yep,' Chris agreed.

'But...' the voice started. 'I know that giving up isn't in your nature.'

'It doesn't matter,' Chris said. 'It doesn't matter if I try or not. Nothing will ever be... good again.'

'But that's nonsense!' the voice said. 'And somewhere deep inside you, you *know* that's nonsense.'

He did. Chris knew that the horrors above would not endure. *Could* not endure. But sometimes life just got a little exhausting. Sometimes people were put under so much pressure that it was impossible to thrive. Sometimes your own mistakes just became too big and infected everything like a disease. Sometimes it seemed impossible to win.

'Stand up,' the voice said.

'Why?' Chris asked.

'Stand up and face it!' the voice demanded. 'You are strong enough to face everything that's out there and more. Think of how far you've come! Others would be envious of your courage. Just because *you* feel like you are failing, doesn't mean that you are! Now get out there and fix it!'

Chris wasn't sure *how* to stand. He wasn't even sure he was really in his body any more. He pulled what he thought of as his leg up at the knee, and placed what he hoped was his left hand onto the floor.

WHICH WAY IS NORTH?

'That's it!' the voice encouraged. 'That's it, Chris! Don't give up!'

He began a sort of swimming motion upwards, and before he knew it, he was back in that same, grey, horrible land. He felt nauseous.

And there in front of him was everything he had dreaded. All of life's problems. And that same grey landscape.

Only, in the distance, he swore he could spot a single, solitary red flower in bloom.

CHRIS MORRIS

The Unlocking

The clouds draw back, the night is long,
No hint of cheer or joy or song,
When out of nowhere bells do chime,
For a glimmer of hope begins to shine…

***

I never wanted this, Derek thought.

It was the latest in a flood of awful thoughts he'd been having lately in relation to his… thing. *I never asked for this* being another common thought, alongside *I'm not the right person, I can't do this,* and *why me?*

Derek was nobody special. At school, he'd been somewhere in between the nerdy type and the guy at the back of the class who nobody expected to particularly excel due to his deep lack of attention. Not really having a clue what to do after school, he'd decided to take a college course in computing (Because it's the future! They said), and graduated four years later. He worked lacklustre jobs within a few different IT departments around town before settling into the one he worked for now at the age of thirty-three: Mega Solutions Inc.

He'd worked there for just over ten years. He would say he hated it if that didn't mean putting more thought into the role than he deemed worthy. He had no close friendships and largely stayed out of office dramas. He felt his colleagues viewed him as a decent enough guy but nothing exciting. He was invited along with the rest of the staff to nights out, and he'd occasionally join them, staying pretty quiet but laughing politely with jokes and making his contribution to rounds of drinks. For Derek, the most exciting yet disheartening thing in his life had been Sarah.

Sarah had started working in Derek's department six months before the day that changed his entire life. His supervisor introduced her to him on a dull Monday morning, and Derek found that he couldn't stop glancing over at her desk for the rest of the day. She seemed always to have a smile on her face and to have an amazing ability to stay relaxed all the time and speak softly, even when she was on the other end of the phone to an irate customer. Derek observed this gleefully about Sarah for the rest of that week, and found himself humiliated every time she asked him for something because he found his heart sped up rapidly, his voice shook as he stuttered out words and he felt out of breath talking to her.

But always, she kept that warm smile and gentle posture. Derek felt like an idiot.

Six months after Sarah started, Derek attended another staff night out at The Ivy, the usual place for the employees of Mega Solutions Inc. He had arrived later than he'd intended, soaked head to toe due to the lashing rain outside. The first full table of his colleagues had laughed when they saw him, and when Derek replaced his glasses after taking them off to remove the rainwater and steam, he saw to his dismay that Sarah was part of this group. The laughter had been in good nature, but there was no seat near her.

'Derek! Over here!'

Steve, perhaps the person in the office Derek was closest to called him over, and he sat with a group of four others a little further away from Sarah.

WHICH WAY IS NORTH?

The night had been uneventful until Derek noticed that Sarah was missing.

He didn't want to make an embarrassing scene out of it. He searched the bar casually, hopeful that he hadn't spotted her somewhere obvious before. Without any success, he finished the last of his drink before telling Steve and the others that he was feeling a little queasy and wanted some fresh air.

Outside, the rain was still hammering down. Derek looked up and down the street but couldn't spot Sarah anywhere. His heart sank.

'Damn...' he whispered.

'Damn?' a bright voice questioned behind him. Derek spun around, and there was Sarah, bright, beautiful smile across her face as usual. 'I was thinking the same myself. Thought you'd gone.'

'Whu..?' Derek stammered. 'Um, me? No! No, I was just getting some fresh air.'

'Oh,' Sarah said. 'Mind if I join you? I've missed you all night!'

'I missed you too.' Derek felt his face turn red as soon as he'd blurted out those stupid words.

What a stupid thing to say. How embarrassing. She thinks you're an idiot. You should probably just go ho... Why is she leaning in towards me?

Her lips were soft, and she kissed him gently with a tenderness that Derek had never known. She had a faint, sweet smell which filled Derek with joy and excitement. But just as he raised his hands to place on Sarah's arms, she stopped suddenly and took his hand in hers.

'Come on,' she said with a look of elation. 'Let's get some privacy.'

They ran through the rain a few streets down, holding hands and giggling like young teenagers. They found an alley which seemed deserted and began to kiss once more. The next few moments would play back in Derek's mind for the rest of his life like a never-ending sordid tale that would perpetually force itself upon him.

The sudden voice. 'Give me your money or I'll stab you.'

The shaking and trembling, not just of Derek but of Sarah too.

The decision to just hand over their wallets.

WHICH WAY IS NORTH?

The refusal from the man to back off. He wasn't satisfied. He wanted to know if they had more.

The moment he stepped towards Sarah, threatening her with the knife.

The moment Derek stepped in, put his hand on the man's shoulder and pulled.

The moment the man thrust the knife forwards, into Sarah's stomach.

The pain in her eyes. Not physical pain. Emotional pain. The gut-wrenching heartache that was felt by both of them.

She fell... Fell into Derek's arms and clutched onto him in a way that made Derek think she was begging him to be

saved. Their eyes met only for a brief moment, and hers said: "help me". He felt utterly powerless.

She slid from Derek and hit the ground, not harshly but gently, as was everything she did in life.

And then in death.

***

When Derek saw the look of veritable indifference on Sarah's killer's face, everything changed.

***

'You killed her!' Derek had screamed. 'You killed Sarah!'

The man had grumbled something inaudible, but his face spoke all the words Derek had needed to hear. A rage had built up inside Derek that would have sent him mad with terror had he been in a position to think clearly. Something inside him had awoken, ignited by the horror and brutality he'd witnessed.

Without thinking much about what he was doing, he punched the man in the stomach. The man flew off his feet and soared through the air to a wall behind him. The wall didn't stop his flight; instead, it crumbled and the man went soaring through it. Derek was too consumed by his own fury to notice how unusual this was and instead pursued his target. If he'd been able to think, he'd have noticed that he covered the distance of about one hundred meters in about six seconds. When he arrived at the bewildered man, he instinctively threw an arm out towards him and what happened next was so bizarre that even in Derek's state of savage rage, he was completely taken aback.

What looked like blue electricity flew from Derek's arm and shot out straight towards the man, whose body writhed horribly as this... force was sent through it. Derek was able to stop it, but the man now lay motionless and covered in the debris from the part of the wall he had just smashed through.

He stood for maybe five minutes trying to comprehend what had just happened. Part of himself wanted to check to see if the man had survived the attack, but another part of himself didn't want to know.

Finally, he called the police. They arrived shortly afterwards to find Sarah's body being carefully cradled by a weeping Derek, who told them that Sarah's killer had run from the scene.

When they found his body, they judged that he'd been killed by a bolt of lightning.

***

They saw him on CCTV. That unearthly punch to the chest that was almost enough to kill the mugger in the first place. That brilliant blue flash of lightning that was a sure kill. And the look of horror on the man's face when he knew what he had done.

He's *perfect.*

They deleted the CCTV footage of course, and when the police had tried to find it and discovered that it had cut around forty-five minutes into the storm, they deduced that, just like the mugger, the cameras had been obliterated by lightning.

Tracing the man had been easy; the computers picked up a clear as daylight image of his face and matched it with an employee at a company called Mega Solutions Inc. They found it just as easy to find his name and then hack into the company's databases to get more information on this *Derek*.

It seemed he was a simple enough man; arrived on time for his job, produced good work and largely kept his head down. No disciplinaries in his entire time there, barely any sick days, and nothing much to talk about. Nothing special.

They would need to contact him quickly, before *the others* did. The others will no doubt have spotted Derek, and might have even managed to see the CCTV footage before it was removed; they had done this sort of thing before. And they had a way of convincing people like Derek that he was important, that he was needed, and that *they* were the side to be on.

It was decided that they should allow him some time to process his grief before they made contact. In the meantime, they would do everything they could to stop the other side from making contact. Indeed, they found that a letter had been sent to his address which looked like one of Derek's regular bills, but an eagle-eyed member spotted a tiny detail on the envelope that was questionable. Deciding that the worst thing that could happen would be for Derek's electricity company to send out a reminder bill, they managed to intercept the letter to find that it did indeed come from the others. They burned it.

They also managed to successfully block electronic signals going to Derek's phone. He missed a few text messages from his friends and family, but everybody just put it down to Derek's sorrow, and nobody questioned it.

All was going well, so far.

The other side seemed to be getting desperate, and they actually sent someone to Derek's door with a handwritten message. As Derek lay in his bed that morning deciding whether or not he would actually get up that day, two women engaged in a secret fight outside his front door. Thankfully for both of them, the front door to Derek's house was tucked away in a nice little corner away from the main road and with only a small amount of houses nearby.

The first woman had a speed so swift that it was matched only by the top athletes in the world, and only when they pushed themselves to their very limit. The other woman had an unbelievable strength matched by nobody else in this world.

They had met in combat twice before, and both times there had been no clear winner. Today, each woman was determined to be the victor, not only because this job was such an incredibly important one, but because (and arguably, *more importantly*) they needed to find out once and for all who was superior.

The woman with super strength was the one from the *other side*, the one trying to deliver the letter to Derek. Her name was Sam, and her rival Jessa charged at her with all the speed she could muster. Seeing her quickly enough, Sam jumped high into the air and aimed a kick at the spot she was sure Jessa's head would be by the time she reached her.

Sam certainly knew her rival well; her foot did indeed make contact with Jessa's mouth, and she fell to the grass outside Derek's flat before swiftly rolling over and standing.

'You're going to have to try harder than that,' Sam said, and she raised her fists to the front of her face in a combat stance, awaiting her opponent's next move.

Jessa wiped some blood from her lower lip. 'Don't get cocky just because you got first blood. Give me the letter and we can both just walk away.'

'Oh?' Sam questioned. 'You don't want to hurt me, is that it? Gained enough respect for me or something stupid like that?'

Sam had barely finished her sentence when in the blink of an eye, Jessa rushed forwards and, spinning on to Sam's back, linked arms and pulled downwards. Sam was too strong for this however, and with a groan, she lunged her arm forwards and sent Jessa crashing to the floor once again. Sam balled a fist and struck downwards, but Jessa moved out of the way and Sam's hand smashed a hole into the ground below.

As Sam cried out in pain, Jessa seized the opportunity to reach quickly into Sam's pocket and seize the letter. She jumped up an inhuman amount into the air and landed softly in a tree, where she showed Sam the letter.

'Give it back!' Sam demanded. 'Don't make me break down that nice tree.'

Before Sam could make any sort of move however, Jessa produced a lighter and set the letter alight.

Sam just looked on calmly. 'You know this doesn't mean you've won, right?'

Jessa nodded. 'You ready?'

'You'd better believe it,' Sam said.

Jessa could have ended it there. She could have returned to her HQ, reported success and received all the praise in the world from her colleagues. But this was Sam. This was personal. This was a question that both of them had been needing answers to for a very long time.

Jessa jumped from the tree, and the pair engaged in battle, one last time.

WHICH WAY IS NORTH?

***

We know what you are.

The words flashed up on Derek's computer screen at work on the first day of his return. They had allowed him a month off alongside a generous counselling programme which Derek had felt wasn't working very well. When he'd arrived at work this morning, everyone had politely smiled or said hello, but largely stayed out of his way. This was to Derek's advantage – he didn't want anyone to see this.

The words had typed themselves onto a Microsoft Word document. Derek had no idea how this could have happened. He began to type a response ("Who is this?" had seemed a good start) but suddenly even more words had begun to appear.

You are not alone. We need you. Meet me tonight and I will explain. I'll send the address to your phone. Don't tell anyone and come alone. Don't worry, we're friends.

Surely enough, the address had been sent to Derek's phone alongside the simple instruction:

9pm.

He'd thought about typing something on his Word document. He'd thought about replying to the text message. But he concluded that whoever these people were, they likely wouldn't engage in a long chat after giving him such direct instructions, so he decided to meet with them.

The address took him to a building in the middle of the city centre. It was tucked away in a quiet-ish part of town in a small alley. Derek double-checked the number and seeing no signage of any sort pressed the buzzer. Nobody spoke, but he heard a soft *click* and found that he was able to push the door open and step inside.

He found a hallway with stairs right in front of him and a small corridor with doors to the side. The door nearest Derek swung open, and an elderly lady stepped out. She had grey hair and a grim look on her face. Her eyes showed a long life lived with much hardship. Derek could tell that she had many stories to tell.

'Derek,' she said. 'Follow me.'

She disappeared through the same door she'd come out of, and Derek followed her in to find a small, comfortable looking room with a large table surrounded by several armchairs. Three men and two women sat there, watching Derek with interest.

'My name is Adelaide,' the old woman said, taking a seat. 'Please, sit down.'

Derek did as he was asked. 'Why did you ask me here? Who are you?'

'Perhaps you should be asking that of yourself,' Adelaide said. 'Who are *you*, really, Derek?'

'I'm nobody,' Derek replied. 'Just an IT man, trying to get by.'

'Funny,' Adelaide said. 'All my years of this life and I've never met a *nobody* before.'

Derek shifted uncomfortably in his seat. The others remained silent but continued looking on at the conversation between Derek and Adelaide with apparent fascination. They didn't look particularly unfriendly, but Derek couldn't be sure whether he was welcome or not.

'Why am I here?' Derek asked again.

'You must know why you're here,' Adelaide said, her old eyes fixed upon Derek. 'You have something. An extraordinary ability. Something you've used only once and have been terrified to try using again since, am I right?'

'How do you know about this?' Derek asked, almost in a whisper.

Adelaide smiled a little. 'Each of us here in this room has abilities. It has been my gift to see them and in some cases know of them before even their hosts did. But none of us have great powers such as the ones you bear, Derek.'

'Look,' Derek began, becoming more alarmed. 'What happened to that man was an accident. I...'

'Of course, Derek,' Adelaide interrupted. 'Of course it was. You had no idea of the power that lurked inside of you, I know you didn't. But now you must try to learn to control it.'

WHICH WAY IS NORTH?

'H-how?' Derek stammered. 'How did I get this... This thing?'

Adelaide closed her eyes and extended both of her open hands towards Derek. The room fell silent. Derek could see her eyelids move as her eyes no doubt darted side to side.

'I think...' Adelaide said, eyes still closed. 'I think there has always been something in you. Yes. Sometimes that's the case. Sometimes our abilities need unlocking. Sometimes a great and terrible thing can be the catalyst. For you, it was a tragedy.'

Sarah... We only had a few minutes together. She was given to me and unjustly taken away in moments. Taken away from everybody – her family, her friends. "Help me" her eyes had begged, and then she was gone.

Adelaide's eyes opened. 'I'm sorry, Derek.' Around the room, the others looked sorrowful.

'These people,' Adelaide said, indicating towards the others in the room. 'They have been waiting. Some of them for their entire lives.'

'Waiting for what?' Derek asked.

'For you,' Adelaide replied.

Derek stood up and began walking towards the door. 'I'm sorry, there must be some mistake. I'm really nobody.'

He placed a hand on the handle, but it wouldn't move.

'Sorry,' one of the men spoke up. 'Adelaide isn't finished yet.'

Derek looked at him in surprise. '*You're* doing this?'

'Please,' the man replied. 'Sit down.'

Derek didn't sit, but he took his hand away from the door and placed it on his head as he started pacing the room. 'I don't understand any of this. A month ago I was living a boring, ordinary life. Then all this happens with Sarah and that rat and... Have I gone crazy?'

Adelaide chuckled slightly. 'No. But I had the same thoughts when I was a little girl and found that I could predict the future. You see Derek, I am one of the people in this room who has been waiting for you for as long as I can remember. It has been foretold that a man with great power would one day come, and bring an end to the darkness.'

WHICH WAY IS NORTH?

'Darkness?' Derek asked with disbelief. 'What darkness?'

'That's a long story,' Adelaide said. 'One that you must hear. For now, all I can say is that long ago there was an omen. That the darkness would come. And it did come, yet only those gifted enough to observe it would be cursed with seeing its true destruction. But the omen also predicted that a light would emerge from among the darkness and that it would guide those gifted people to victory.'

Adelaide stood slowly now and walked over to Derek. She held both of his hands in hers, gently.

'You must have courage now Derek,' she said. 'I wish I had the time to tell you more, but my time grows short.'

'What do you mean?' Derek asked.

Adelaide smiled softly once more. 'My gift of seeing the future comes with a grave misfortune. I tried to run away from it for many years, but finally the date of my own death became known to me. I'm rather afraid our meeting tonight is to be very short-lived.'

And even as she said these words, Derek saw that she was becoming weaker. Her cold hands trembled and her legs began to give way. Derek did his best to support her tenderly to her seat again. The others in the room had risen to their feet in concern as they watched.

'Derek,' Adelaide said. 'Don't be afraid. You must lead these people now, not me. Everything you've ever known and more is at stake.'

Derek felt tears come to his eyes. 'I can't! I don't even know these people! I don't know what this darkness you're talking about is. I'm nobody special, nobody at all!'

'If you can't find a way,' Adelaide said. 'Then I fear nobody will.'

Adelaide closed her eyes, and Derek and the others stayed with her until the end.

***

I never wanted this, Derek thought.

I wish it had never come to me, this wretched power.

Damn it! Damn this thing!!

How did Adelaide know I'm definitely the one the omen foretold of?

Yet, here he was. Derek the IT man, in charge of a band of... superheroes? Fighting a thing called the darkness. The years ahead would be tough, and Derek strode forwards with a growing determination.

All he could do was learn to use his powers, find out all he could about this "darkness" and do his best to stop it. At least it made his life more exciting, he supposed.

He began to feel confident that he knew his place, and he knew what it was he was supposed to do.

Until he received a handwritten letter in the post.

A letter that read:

Dear Derek,

Everything you were told by Adelaide was a lie. You are being manipulated. DO NOT go back to the HQ. I will meet you tonight when it's safe.

Your friend,

S.

***

His mind was teeming, his spirit low,
How should he proceed? Who is his foe?
The bells are quelled, the clouds are full,
Deeds performed by a ghastly ghoul…

CHRIS MORRIS

Contingency Plan

She's getting away, Luke desperately thought as he pursued the athletic woman down the bustling street.

His lungs ached from the effort he had been putting into the chase. His target was fast – much faster than any he'd seen before. He worried that he might not catch up with her and what that would mean. He decided to put that to the back of his mind and focus on telling his legs to propel him forwards as fast as they could manage.

The street was busy, and the woman running away from Luke was about a hundred meters away. Luke had already barged awkwardly past many strangers without having the required breath to whisper an apology. Ahead of him, he spotted half a dozen other potential hazards and to his great surprise, managed to form a half decently helpful list in a matter of seconds. His exact thoughts went something like this:

WHICH WAY IS NORTH?

1. Woman being pulled across my path by a large dog (breed unknown to me, I'm not a dog person), which has spotted the obviously familiar butcher's shop and is keen to be admired by the butcher (who is a dog person) to the point of receiving a free slice of something. Dogs. Some people would do anything for them based solely on their cute, smiling faces and excited, wagging tails. Me, I can't imagine being okay with having to walk them and pick up their poo multiple times a day.

2. Man doing that stupid thing that people do; waving goodbye to his friend on the other side of the street and walking backwards as he does so. Why do people do that? Have they forgotten that they can't see behind them? Do they expect everyone else to just move out of their way? Are they... Okay, okay, no time for this. Move on.

3. Bus pulling in to a bus stop just a few meters ahead. It will open its doors and an unknown number of people will step off and flood the streets with even more *people. Some of them will do that annoying thing that people do when they get off the bus. You know, they'll walk a few steps ahead and then stop in the middle of the street looking up and down as if they're trying to remember where it is they are supposed to be going. People do that at the top/bottom of escalators too, like they can't comprehend that there might be a load of people behind them who CAN'T STOP to allow them a few seconds of standing there deciding where it is they're going. I mean – oh, yeah, the rest of the list. Focus, Luke!*

4. Painter with paint pot balanced unnervingly close to the end of a scaffolding tower. This one's a bit of a long shot, but you never know. One wrong move from the painter and that pot will go hurtling towards the ground, and aside from being embarrassingly covered in paint (a kind of lime green, in case you were wondering), the pot could still be heavy enough to do some real damage if it fell on me.

5. Two men carefully carrying a large sheet of glass into a store that needs a new window. Just kidding! How cliché in this situation! FOCUS, LUKE!!

Real number 5. The woman I'm chasing is approaching a road in front of us, and the green man is still on but flashing, indicating that the dastardly red man will arrive very soon and the road between me and her will fill with traffic. It would be slightly humiliating if I sprint towards that road and have to stop and wait patiently for the green man to come back before galloping off again. I could maybe do that running on the spot thing that joggers do at roads they're waiting to cross, but being dressed in trousers and a shirt and jumper I may look slightly odd.

*   6. A grand piano being lifted up to a high flat via a worryingly thin piece of rope which looks very frayed. STOP IT, LUKE!!*

*   Real number 6. A small child, female, possibly around three years old. She's holding her father's hand, but she's spotted number one – the dog – and she's thinking about stopping not very far in front of me to watch it as it pulls its owner eagerly towards that butcher shop. Why do all kids act like they've never seen a dog before? I've not counted, but I can almost guarantee that I've seen at least ten of them just today. People are dog mad, I don't get it.*

Luke smiled to himself; he was pleased by how quickly his mind was able to put together a list like this one. It reminded him of his crowning achievement; the solution to *The Subway Situation.* That had been a real biggie. He'd began to be more cost-efficient, but standing in line at his local Subway one afternoon, his mind had drifted and he found himself dreaming of his usual meatball sandwich.

He could almost remember the feeling now as he raced across the street towards the woman. That stomach rumbling, the sudden realisation of hunger and the eager anticipation of the tender, tasty meatballs in their nice sauce.

When he'd been asked what he would like, he began: 'Meeeeeaaaa...' before realising that it was one of the most expensive sandwiches on the menu, having a quick and efficient panic attack and successfully turning his sentence into something other than "meatball".

'Mmmmeeeeee? Sorry, were you speaking to me?'

The server had looked at him with a bewildered expression. 'Erm... yes. What would you like?'

And here, Luke had once again stupidly forgotten about his new saving money policy.

'Mmmmm...(!)'

Damn it, damn it, damn it! How can I turn this into something else? Could pretend I was just saying "mmmm!" in anticipation of a tasty meal? No! That would be stupid. What kind of sandwich could I order that is cost-effective, tasty and begins with "M"?

Mmmm... Mince? No!

WHICH WAY IS NORTH?

Mmmm... Mint? Don't be stupid!!

Mmmm... Marmalade? Oh, you're just getting ridiculous now. Who are you, Paddington Bear? If there's not already one tucked underneath your bucket hat, you don't need one.

Oh, I know!

'Mmmmm...' Luke had continued again. 'Mmmmaaayyy I please have...'

Cracked it! Except, now you've got to think about what you want to order. May you please have what, *Luke?*

'...Yes?' the server had tried to encourage a decision.

'May I please have...' Luke repeated. 'A six-inch chicken breast?'

Anyone who had entered Luke's mind would have considered this a roaring success. However, Luke couldn't help but wonder whether the server had possibly thought that Luke was asking for a precise size of chicken breast, instead of the size of his sandwich.

All things considered, Luke had impressed himself by how well he'd handled *The Subway Situation*.

His mind turned back to the current situation of the race towards the woman.

Pleased with his list, and keeping the woman within his sights, Luke decided now that he would have to come up with an action plan. Actually, action wasn't quite the right word for it, and it also got a stupid song stuck in his head. *Aaaction plan, the greatest hero of them alll!* He pondered for a moment when the last time that advert would have been on TV, metaphorically slapped his wrist for rhyming *man* with *plan*, then concluded that "contingency plan" was a better phrase to use for this situation.

His contingency plan went like this:

1. The woman with the dog is already moving fast enough to be out of my way by the time I reach her. Even if the dog wasn't pulling hard, she'd be at the doorstep of the butcher shop in two seconds. If I could turn back time and remove this from my original hazard list ("Hazard list"... I didn't actually call it that but that's a good name), I would.

2. Man walking backwards. What's that thing that runners shout when they're on the track and they're passing

WHICH WAY IS NORTH?

another runner? I'll shout that. Slight problem, I don't remember what the word is. Also, this guy might not be a track runner and would have no clue why I'm shouting whatever it is I'm shouting. Easy solution – I'll shout "On your left!" like that scene in Captain America because everyone's seen the Marvel movies, right?

3. Bus about to unload a tonne of passengers. I've already brushed past a fair few pedestrians and getting lightly knocked into doesn't seem to be a problem with most of them. However, if I knock a little too harshly into someone, they might get a bit upset, and they might chase me. But this is to my advantage, as it will only make me run faster. I don't think there's an issue here any more.

4. If that pot of paint falls I'm almost certain I can catch it by the handle and fling it back up towards the painter who will catch it easily and give me an encouraging thumbs-up as I run towards my target. Easy. Move on.

5. Green man moving to a red man. I estimate that I can either get to that road just in time for the green man to be allowing the last of the pedestrians across, or I'll miss it by the skin of my teeth. Skin of the teeth – what does that even mean? To the best of my knowledge, teeth don't have skin. I accept I could be wrong about that (Biology wasn't my best subject at school), but I really don't think I am. Anyway... green man situation! The worst-case scenario would be that I arrive there just as a car is beginning to drive again after waiting at the red light – that means the fastest the car could be driving would be something like ten miles an hour. Fifteen at most. I think that's a safe enough speed to pull off that thing they do in action movies all the time, you know, when they slide along the bonnet of the car. They might blast their horn at me, but I'll never see them again (probably), so it's worth the few seconds of embarrassment.

6. What was number six again? Damn it, Luke, think! Ah! Of course! The piano. That's such a cartoonish situation I must have imagined it. Nothing to worry about there.

He couldn't stop himself from metaphorically patting himself on the back. Hell, he might have *literally* patted himself on the back if that wouldn't interfere with his hopefully perfectly timed plan.

His plan, actually, reminded him of a contingency plan that he'd come up with a few years before that he was proud of. It was a bit of a silly one really, but he had concluded that nobody really knows if or when you might need such a plan.

It was his evacuation plan from his university's library in the event of a sudden zombie outbreak.

He had counted the windows in the library and judged which of these might be safe to jump from (given that the library was up on the second floor). Only two of these he had deemed "safe", three were "dangerous", and one was "the same as suicide". The safe ones were so labelled because one of them had a patch of soft bushes directly underneath and the other had a tree next to it that could easily be reached. The three dangerous ones were straight drops, and Luke determined that he'd only have a 37.6% (or so) chance of hitting the ground without any injuries, minor or otherwise. The last window was labelled so harshly not because of the distance to the floor below, but because it was situated right next to the grumpy librarian who would shoosh Luke at the slightest hint of his humming his favourite tune while he studied. She'd probably get him in trouble, zombie apocalypse or no zombie apocalypse, for daring to noisily open her window for escape (and on a cold day too).

CHRIS MORRIS

Aside from the assessment of windows, Luke would each day take a mental note of the other library users and determine which of them he could possibly outrun. Assessing the fitness levels and possible speed of each person in the library was important, and for differing reasons depending on what *kind* of zombies we were talking about. If it was the classic, George Romero zombie, then a low fitness level from his competitors – sorry, *other library users* – was favourable, because then Luke had a good chance of outrunning them while they fell prey to the mindless monsters. However, if there were zombies like the ones in *28 Days Later* (Okay, these technically weren't *zombies* in the traditional sense but let's just go with it), then a low fitness level from the other people in the library became doubly important; while it was still the case that Luke had a better chance of outrunning them, it was also probable that even when these people were caught and turned into the super-zombie types that can run after you, they would still be slower than him, and he could make a good attempt at getting away.

WHICH WAY IS NORTH?

Luke had allowed himself a small, satisfied chuckle once his zombie contingency plan had been solidified.

'*Sssshhhh!!*' the grumpy librarian had said.

Luke had determined: *Fitness level: three out of ten. Lowest one here.*

And he had allowed himself one more chuckle, low enough to be under the radar of the librarian's nuisance noise detector.

Satisfied with his present contingency plan, Luke found a new sense of confidence and urged himself forwards. His heart pounded faster yet, but Luke enjoyed the sensation of it, assured that he was on his way to achieving his goal of catching the woman in front. He was gaining on her too, and he began to feel a great sense of excitement at the idea of catching up.

He soared past the woman with the dog who, as he'd predicted, was already at the doorstep of the butchers; the dog with a look of excited anticipation on its face as the woman struggled to keep it from pulling her off her feet.

Not for me, Luke thought. *I really don't get the dog thing.*

The man walking backwards finished his goodbye and Luke drew a breath in to make his shout. He was cut short when the man's friend on the other side of the street shouted 'Oh! By the way!', making the man with his back turned to Luke pause just long enough for him to slip behind him unnoticed and with no need for any action.

When the bus stopped and opened its doors, nobody got off. As he passed, Luke joined the queue of people at the bus stop waiting to get on as they looked in at an elderly woman shouting at the driver about braking too harshly and something about her false teeth falling out. Luke couldn't help but allow himself a small smile of satisfaction before sprinting on.

She's closer now. I'm gaining!

Looking upwards at the paint pot, he saw the slightest wobble before it settled back into position. Fate was with him! Nothing could stop him now! He'd overcome every obstacle placed in front of him, and now the only thing for it was to…

The child!!

WHICH WAY IS NORTH?

The piano was made up to satisfy Luke's stupid humour going on inside his head. Of course it was. But his mind had overwritten the actual problem of the little girl who had spotted the dog heading into the butcher shop (surely all that would be left to see now was an excited wagging tail? Kids!). Luke should have blocked the cartoon thoughts from his head completely and focussed on this little girl. Now his head would really have to get to work.

Alright, alright, don't panic. Little girl. Age: three? Height: about three feet two. State: completely distracted by the cute dog that's wandering into the butchers hoping for a lamb chop or a T bone steak or a whole turkey… whatever it is that those dog thingies get. She seems totally unaware of her other surroundings and will most definitely walk straight into my path even if her father can keep hold of her hand. He looks like he ought to manage that no problem; he's about six feet tall and looks to be gripping on tightly enough to his daughter's hand that she would have to be covered in some sort of slippy goo (which a three-year-old might well be) in order to break free.

There's only one way out of this. Me, I'm five feet ten, thirteen stone, and only about sixty-seven per cent fatigued by the run so far. I estimate that if I time this just right (two more steps should do it I think), I can get past this child safely and easily…

Two steps later, Luke bent his knees into position before extending and leaping as high as he could into the air. He soared above the girl like a kangaroo, the wind from his movement just enough to ruffle her hair as she kept her gaze fixed upon the cute little doggy she wanted to point out to her father. The father was among several others who looked in bewilderment and with a hint of awe towards the airborne Luke as he cleared the small child with plenty space to spare and landed sure-footedly on the pavement in front with barely a wobble before continuing his sprint onwards.

And here, finally, Luke caught up with his target. The green man had actually gone and was replaced by the red man before the woman had arrived at the road.

Gather your breath, Luke. This is it.

Trying to breathe more slowly so that his speech was something like English, Luke slowed to a walk and approached the woman he'd been chasing.

WHICH WAY IS NORTH?

'S'cuse me,' he panted, and the woman turned around.

She was beautiful. Her long hair was tied elegantly behind her head to reveal a lovely shape of a face with sparkling green eyes and the warmest smile Luke thought he'd ever seen. He suddenly felt quite nervous.

'Um...'

Don't act like an idiot, just tell her!

The woman stood patiently, looking at Luke with a slightly puzzled expression. Luke held up the item in his hand. 'I think you dropped this.'

The woman looked at what Luke was holding, and her face turned to one of pure gratitude.

'Oh my god!' she said. 'I can't believe I dropped it, I feel like an idiot. Thank you so much!'

Luke was holding out a phone inside a case which also looked to be holding several cards and was jingling with coins. The woman held out her hand to take it, and her fingertips brushed Luke's. He felt a pleasant shiver run down his body.

CHRIS MORRIS

This is a brief, chance encounter with a woman who could be your soul mate. She's beautiful, and she looks kind and warm and clever. You hear stories about this sort of thing. Married couples revealing they met in the most ludicrous ways. Maybe this is it. Maybe I should ask for her number. What's the harm? She says no and you never see her again, life moves on. She says yes and...

'Hey, um...' Luke started with a slightly shaky voice. 'I'm Luke. I was wondering...'

She'd taken the phone by this point, and Luke had spotted a photograph that had been inserted into the back of it. It was of her, but she wasn't alone. Luke's heart sank.

'Yeah?' the woman asked, still smiling.

'Is that your dog? In the picture?'

She looked at the back and her smile widened. She chuckled. 'Yeah. That's Ollie. I've had him for three years now. Is... that what you wanted to ask me?'

'Yeah,' Luke said almost instantly. Now he just wanted to get away. 'Well, be careful with your phone! Enjoy your run!'

WHICH WAY IS NORTH?

Luke turned away before he could see the disappointment in the woman's face. His dejection was so strong he felt the need to close his eyes as he walked away. If he'd only opened them, he would have spotted the two men holding the large plate of glass before he bumped awkwardly into it.

CHRIS MORRIS

My Hero

As I sit in front of my piano in my dimly lit study, my fingers tremble. It's a gloomy, rainy night and I am alone. There's nobody around. So why is it that I'm so nervous to start work on my first original composition?

Perhaps I'm afraid the sound of my piano will carry further through the walls of my own house, and I'll disturb my neighbours. Perhaps I fear it's late, and I'll be too tired to compose. Ultimately I *know* what the issue is. I am afraid of one of the deepest of all human anxieties.

I am afraid that I'll fail.

Even though nobody else need hear the melodies, I attempt to create on this black and white engineer of song. I might fashion some of the worst music in history tonight, but nobody will hear it, and nobody will know how truly abysmally I failed.

But *I* will. I will know I have failed and I will live with that. I will walk into my study and look ashamedly out of the corner of my eye at the piano gathering dust in the corner and know how awfully I was beaten. And it will infect other areas of my life; I will never succeed in my job, I will never have meaningful relationships with other human beings, and I will live my life *safely*, afraid to step even lightly into the spotlight of ambition, my only desire to live life with my head down and my path set in dark stone ahead of me.

At times like these, it helps me to remember Miriam.

Miriam was my piano teacher at school many years ago. She was an elderly woman close to retirement. She always had a smile on her face and a kind remark at hand. Her gentle eyes sparkled with familiar welcome each time I entered her small classroom and for the half-hour or so that we had our lesson (*our* lesson mind you, Miriam would always say, "because I learn just as much from you as you do from I"), I would forget the stresses of due homework for other classes, the social pressures facing most teenagers going through school, and all the turbulent family issues that plagued the day.

Piano lessons were without a doubt the best part of school.

CHRIS MORRIS

I remember Miriam once asked me to perform at the school's annual talent show. Beethoven's *Bagatelle in C*. I was terrified, and Miriam knew it.

'It's okay,' she'd said with her signature warm smile. 'It's completely fine to be nervous. Don't try not to be, it'll only make you *more* nervous. I wouldn't have put you forward if I didn't already know that you'll be fantastic.'

But my anxiety would only deepen over the weeks leading up to the performance. I regretted telling Mum and Dad about it because they were so enthusiastic and excited to come and hear me play. Even my English teacher caught wind of my imminent appearance on stage and promised to be there in the audience, listening to every note.

In my last lesson before the big night, Miriam saw how nervous I was, and I received the most helpful piano lesson of my time at school. She told me the story of her own first performance.

Miriam hadn't been particularly privileged as a child. She'd grown up in a family that wasn't poor, but certainly couldn't afford a frivolous and exorbitant activity such as music lessons. If it weren't for her own music teacher at school, she would never have learned an instrument at all. Miriam's music teacher had a strong belief that every child should have the opportunity to learn an instrument, and would offer those who couldn't afford lessons to stay behind after school to learn piano with her for free.

Miriam was inspired by her teacher and quickly found confidence in her abilities, thanks in part to her own particular talent, but more so to her teacher who showed incredible patience and encouragement. She had progressed quickly, and by the time she had left school she had a Grade 8 qualification in piano, with distinction no less.

The most important thing throughout all of this, Miriam told me, was that nobody thought she could do it. Her friends and her family had all but laughed at her when she'd told them about learning piano. *You're from a working-class family,* they'd said. *You have to be clever to learn piano.* Her entire musical journey was fraught with doubt and snobbish pretension. I can only imagine how difficult it must have been for her.

CHRIS MORRIS

The only person who had believed in Miriam had been her teacher. And what an important thing that was for Miriam. If, in a world inhabited by one billion people, all but one of them tell you that they have no faith in you, then that one in one billion becomes the most incredibly motivating, influential and important number in existence. That number was Miriam's teacher.

Passing her Grade 8 exam had filled Miriam with such confidence and happiness that it became her path in life. She had a profound passion for piano, but even more zeal for passing on to others what her teacher had given her – confidence in herself. When Miriam sat me down in that piano room to explain her story, I felt enormous pride in being one of her students. She told me it was simply the story of how she became a teacher. I thought of it as her superhero origin story, because how different was it to the story of an ordinary person who discovers abilities they have hidden within them and decides to use these abilities for good? Miriam was my hero.

But perhaps an even better display of Miriam's heroism was the story of her first ever performance. A few years before her success in her Grade 8 exam,

WHICH WAY IS NORTH?

Miriam's teacher had invited her to perform at a twice-annual concert that she used to run for her private students. Asking a student who was receiving free, after-school lessons to play at one of these concerts wasn't usual, but Miriam was told that her teacher had seen so much potential in her that she thought a public performance would set her on the path to something special.

And Miriam's chosen piece for this performance was none other than *Bagatelle in C*.

Listening to Miriam's story, I expected to hear that she was nervous, perhaps even to the point where she didn't want to play at all, but that she had overcome it and performed the piece so well that Beethoven himself would have enthusiastically applauded. But the story was quite different to that.

The performance started well enough; she struck out the opening chords confidently and accurately, but the moment she accidentally hit a D sharp instead of a D, the nerves set in and she began playing more wrong notes, making the chords clash in jarring mistakes. Dynamics were completely abandoned, and Miriam played the rest of the piece at a volume so low that those in the back must have had to have strained to hear her.

Once I tried to stop myself from being nervous, it just made things worse, Miriam had told me. *The more I let my heart get out of control, the more my fingers were out of control.*

But incredibly, at the end of what Miriam thought of as a terrible performance, the audience warmly applauded and her teacher smiled happily and congratulated her with a pat on the back. She had thought for a while that this was only faux praise, a sympathetic pat on the back to say *don't worry, we can't all be good at things.* But in her next lesson with her piano teacher, she was told that her bravery was admirable, and the fact that she had kept playing through her mistakes and hadn't just stopped and walked off the stage was a sign of someone trying their utmost, and simply getting a little first performance nerves. All the makings of a future star, Miriam had been told, were on display for the world to see, and nobody could have given more than that.

Even superheroes, it seemed to me, could make mistakes. Even superheroes can get nervous, be imperfect, only to later rise to become the people that those closest to them have always known they are.

Going into that talent show, I felt much more confident in myself. I was still incredibly nervous, but I remembered what Miriam had said to me:

Don't try not to be nervous. It'll only make you more nervous.

So I allowed the nerves to be a part of me on the stage. I didn't look into the audience to spot my parents, or Miriam, or even my old English teacher who promised she'd be watching. I sat in front of that old school piano, took a deep breath and performed Beethoven's piece to the best of my ability. When it was done, I received all the praise in the world from my peers and my teachers. And the look of pride on Miriam's face was enough for a single wet tear to run down my cheek and be quickly brushed away before anyone could notice.

That important day led me to where I am right now, here in my study on this rainy night, fingers delicately resting on the keys of my piano and wondering where on earth I can begin. The memories of my old teacher rushing through my head have filled me with both joy and sadness, because I heard that Miriam passed away last year. There was a small obituary in the local newspaper:

Suddenly but peacefully at home, surrounded by family. Beloved mother, grandmother and wife. Cherished music teacher for over fifty years. Piano is all black and white, but life isn't. It's up to us to navigate it, and may we do it well.

That last part was something Miriam was known to say often to her students, and was embossed on her grave in the cemetery. I cried when I read it, but I also smiled. I smiled because I knew that so many others would read that and know that it was something she used to say, and that they would hold it close to them throughout their lives. It would help shape the direction they took and perhaps would shine even the smallest glimpse of light on a dark day.

My story is different from Miriam's. I did not choose to pursue a career in music. My life took another path. But her lessons hold true and dear to me today, and composing a song on piano reminds me that I am capable of achieving great things. And that is an important thing that we must all remind ourselves of from time to time. And sometimes it takes a hero of a person to do that for us.

I will proceed with confidence. I will sit at this piano in front of me, and I will write a composition. I'm not sure exactly how it will go yet, but I believe I'll call it *My Hero*, and it will be a tribute to one of the most important people in my life.

Thank you, Miriam. The world needs heroes like you.

CHRIS MORRIS

What If?

Jane Wright hated her house. It was a big, useless, cluttered mishmash of *things*. There was so much that everything had to be crammed, stuffed and shoved into every nook and cranny. She often thought of hiring a skip to take all of it away, but every time this thought arrived in her busy mind she found that she just couldn't bear to part with all of the house's things.

All of the memories, bleak as they were.

Yet for all the sheer amount of items in her large house, the place felt absolutely empty. The house was situated in the woods, miles away from the city. It had been under her family's ownership for over two hundred years, and in that time it had been shaped and reshaped in many different ways. Extensions had been built both on the ground level and above, and the house had ended up three floors high with new rooms jutting outwards here and there giving the place a mad, untidy look. Jane had once thought of it as a fairytale castle, but no tale

WHICH WAY IS NORTH?

happy enough to be thought of in such a way had ever taken place here.

Sitting now in her old bedroom, she opened her bedside drawer and had one of those strange moments; when your mind goes somewhere, arrives at an idea of something that needs doing, or remembers where something you were looking for might be, and then queerly forgets it. Sometimes this happens because we find something that distracts our thought process, and this certainly had just happened to Jane because she found an old photograph in the drawer that she had forgotten was there. Picking it up and looking at it with scorn for a mere few seconds, she tore it into pieces. She slowly walked over to her bedroom window before opening it and throwing the components of the photograph out into the decrepit back garden. They floated more gracefully than a sordid, black memory like that one deserved, and landed next to the frame of a very old and battered kite that had tangled its string around the unruly shrubs and had refused to fly away, choosing instead to sit there as a constant reminder to Jane that she can close her eyes, she can turn away, but she can never outrun her own past.

Sometimes Jane stood at this window to try and see something, *anything* in her surroundings that wasn't so full of sadness or anger. It was foolish; yes the house was full of objects that might once have brought happiness and now contained the memories of a life that never really was, but she would see nothing different outside of her bedroom window, or any window in this lonely place. The overgrown garden was a reminder of her failure to keep the things in her life under control, the grand driveway at the front of the house an empty memory that she was alone now, and that this was unlikely to change. Even the trees of the forest around her seemed to whisper forbidden echoes etched into time, telling her that they too had witnessed every moment of her time here. Every deed. Every failure.

She hadn't always lived in this house alone. At its busiest time, the place had been home to seven Wrights and one other. Jane had inherited her home from her parents. She had lived in the house for her entire life, birth to now, an elderly woman with too many sad memories. She had met Hugh in her early twenties, and by the time they'd married, Jane's mother had passed away and the couple moved in with Jane's father, Edward.

The look on his face!

Jane was startled. 'Hello? Who's there?'

Oh, sorry. You can hear me?

'Yes, I can hear you,' Jane said, voice shaking slightly. She looked around her room. 'Who are you?'

Oh, you won't see me. You can stop looking around. I've been with you for your entire life.

Jane shuddered but tried not to let the fear show in her voice when she spoke. 'What do you mean?'

It's okay. Ah, go back to the memories. This place is full of them. Where did we get to? Yes! The look on his face! Hugh's, I mean. When you told him you weren't leaving the family home, and neither was your father, Edward. So if he wanted to live with you, he'd have to live with him too. It was almost as good as when you told him you wouldn't take his surname, and that he'd have to have yours!

'Leave me alone!' Jane wailed, and she stood up and moved out of her bedroom as quickly as she could, slamming the door behind her. Dust fell from the door frame and lay next to all the rest of the debris on the carpet below.

Her bedroom was on the third floor, and in her old age it had begun to burden her. She'd have moved into a bedroom on the second floor, but three of her four children had occupied bedrooms there, and she dared not go in. Those memories would sting like a poisoned arrow aimed consciously at what was left of her fractured heart.

She moved instead into the study. In here was a large bookshelf filled to the brim with academic books on the subject of everything from science to the study of classical music. These books were very old, and Jane had always assumed that her ancestors perhaps liked to look like they were well-read, because they were covered in dust so thick that Jane often wondered what memories this dust itself had stored in its being. Hugh had gone through a spell of picking up a few of these books with a faux interest in their content. Still, he had given up quite quickly, leaving Jane with yet more bad memories to contend with.

WHICH WAY IS NORTH?

More books lay strewn untidily across the floor, sprawled next to a desk with an old PC which looked slightly out of place among the more traditional look of the room. Several pictures hung on the wall. They had been there, Jane thought, for as long as she had lived in the house and they looked to be original artwork. Scenes of beautiful countrysides, vast oceans and blizzardy mountain ranges in places of the world she'd only ever dreamed of.

She sat at the desk with the computer and tried to regain her composure, but perhaps the computer wasn't the best place to be. Agnes had liked to use this computer a lot. She used to sit for hours at a time in this very room, on this same chair, until Elise was able to pull her away from it and do something fun with her outside.

Perhaps if she just sat there a while, and tried to think of something else…

You can't outrun me, Jane.

She jumped when she heard it. Worried that her voice would disclose her fright, she said nothing.

Let's talk, you and I. How long has it been now? Since you were left alone in this house? Twenty years? And not once in that time have you thought about pruning the hedges? Planting flowers to replace the ones that died because you never watered them? When are you planning on weeding? The gardens are horrible. They used to be so beautiful, back in the day. Don't you remember? Everything was so neatly trimmed, and the residents used to love walking the pathways and sitting out on the benches to read in the summer. You could have at least cut down the rope swing after...

'Enough!' Jane shouted, and with all her effort she stood, fury-filled eyes darting around the room looking for any clue as to where this (Person? Ghost?) was.

I'm sorry. I struck a nerve there, didn't I? Truthfully, I'm sorry. These painful memories you have – they plague me too. Tell me something, Jane. You're planning on leaving, aren't you?

Jane caught her breath and slowly lowered herself back on to the chair. 'Yes,' she whispered. 'Tomorrow.'

Ah. You haven't packed a thing.

'No.' Because how could she? What would she pack? Every last cursed thing in this house held so much despair. The hidden photographs, the discarded books, the little unwashed pair of Wellington boots downstairs, the old, thick pair of glasses on the mantelpiece above the fire, the tiny scratch marks on door frames, the fading ghostly footprints on the paths outside, and that horrid, wretched kite in the garden that should have blown away years ago.

Have you ever inspected that thing closely? It may have left... something on it. Something not nice at all. Maybe it's best you don't. Have you ever wondered where everything started to go wrong?

She supposed it had all come to boiling point when her fourth child, Jacob, was born.

Ah, yes, Jacob. He was a good boy - poor, sweet soul.

'You're really able to listen in to my thoughts?' Jane asked aloud, finding it strange that she had chosen to do so given what they were discussing.

Of course I can. Please, just continue your thoughts. Pretend I'm not here.

(*Like you've done your entire life.*)

Jacob... When Jane had found out she was pregnant with him, she and Hugh had decided that this would be their last child. Jane hadn't planned on it being the final straw in a struggling marriage. Hugh had been wonderful at first; almost the perfect husband. He'd worked very hard and had been promoted to a high position in his company but still found time for Jane and looked after the house as though it had been in his own family for centuries.

A few months after their marriage, Jane fell pregnant with their first child, a boy they'd named Malcolm. Malcolm had been a boisterous child but had grown up with a loving and supportive mother, father and grandfather. Edward had relaxed somehow when Malcolm was born. Jane thought he was probably relieved to see another Wright in the family house. More blood that could inherit the old place and pass it on to new generations down the line.

Five years later Jane and Hugh had twin girls, Agnes and Elise. It was then that the first signs of trouble began.

What! Because of the girls? You don't mean that, surely? What a fine pair they were!

They were, of course they were. Sweet little things who could do no harm. But they weren't the problem.

No. You had two problems then.

WHICH WAY IS NORTH?

Edward and Hugh.

Which one do you want to talk about first?

Edward. Dad... He fell very ill. His mind wasn't what it was before. He started forgetting things. Little things at first. Things that we all do from time to time. He misplaced his house keys, he forgot about appointments. But Jane had become most concerned when he started forgetting things like which bedroom was his, and what the name of his first grandchild was. Naturally, she went to Hugh for support and comfort in this time, only...

Only he didn't seem to care, did he? He'd been drinking. Coming home at night in a state that caused you so much concern. This house being where it is, he'd have driven too. You fought him about it, afraid your father would hear the squabbles. But then, what if he did? Would he have even had the sense to know that you were fighting?

'Stop it!' Jane spat. 'What a horrible, nasty thing to say!'

Oh. I'm sorry. I'm not used to speaking to people. I've been alone longer than you have.

'What are you? A ghost? A spirit of some kind?'

No, I'm not dead. I was never truly alive, to begin with. And I've never been what you'd describe as a person.

'What then?' Jane demanded.

That would take a long time to explain. It's complicated. A story for another time perhaps. I interrupted you, and it's very much your story. Your thoughts that you should get out before you leave this place. Please, continue.

Hugh became more distant as the years drew on, and Edward became more ill. He was often locked inside his own room for entire days before Jane would practically force him out to spend some time with his family. Despite the problematic relationship she had with Hugh, Jane was able to find moments of joy with him, sparse as they were. She believed that if she just didn't lose hope, Hugh would come around and be the man she loved again. Jane waited, but nothing changed for many years.

Malcolm was nine, and the girls were four when Rebecca came into their lives.

Rebecca. My goodness, Jane. I can feel you spit out that name like a nasty parasite that's somehow crept its way into your mouth.

WHICH WAY IS NORTH?

'Can you blame me for that?' Jane asked without anger.

No.

Thinking about the sob story that Hugh had presented at the time made Jane feel foolish. Rebecca had been a young woman who had worked with Jane's husband, and Hugh had claimed that she had suddenly found herself with nowhere to go. Something about an abusive relationship and how she had found herself with no family to go to and no friends to rely on. Jane had eventually been convinced to allow her one of the spare rooms until she could get herself back on her feet.

It had been the first time, Edward claimed, that a person without the surname of Wright had lived in the house for nearly one hundred and fifty years. Jane had caught Hugh rolling his eyes at this, but she'd decided not to make an argument out of it.

When Jane had met Rebecca, the woman had been excessively nice to her. Full of all the "thank you"s and "I can't believe someone would do this for me"s that a person could give. Jane couldn't argue that they didn't have the space for her, and she didn't want to seem uncharitable to a woman who had been nothing but pleasant to her. She was quite possibly escaping a dangerous situation, so she had reluctantly agreed while knowing somewhere inside of her that this was wrong.

Rebecca stayed in the house for six years. She had...

Sorry. I'm sorry for interrupting again, but six years! How did you let it happen? Why didn't you do something about it?

'Oh, Hugh and I had our fights about it. Of course, I never suspected anything was going on between them until much later.'

Idiot.

'Excuse me!?' Jane didn't try to conceal the anger in her voice.

Oh, come on, Jane! You're thinking it too. You're calling yourself an idiot in your own mind. Have done for years. A young, pretty woman just rolling up to your house and staying there with her "best friend", your husband for six years. It's almost entirely unbelievable! I'm sorry if I've offended you but...

WHICH WAY IS NORTH?

'You're having to make an awful lot of apologies tonight,' Jane pointed out.

Yes. Six long years though. My goodness.

At the end of those six years, Jacob was born and things went really badly. Malcolm, being fifteen at this point, was able to show a level of maturity, and Agnes and Elise were always pleasant enough about it. But nobody could stop s*taring.*

Yourself included. What was it called again? Jacob's condition?

'Polymelia.'

Yes, polymelia. It affected people in slightly different ways, but it always means the same thing: at least one extra limb. In Jacob's case, it was an extra leg, shrunken and deformed, jutting awkwardly outwards in a position which Jane thought looked uncomfortable. On the day of his birth, Jane had held him tightly and couldn't stop pondering about his future and what the kids at school would say. She had thousands of arguments with thousands of imaginary children in preparation for what she foresaw in Jacob's life. She was ready to take them all on. What she hadn't planned for was a fight with his own father.

Hugh couldn't accept it. He'd looked down on his son with a revulsion which turned Jane's stomach and twisted her heart. He consistently made flippant, appalling remarks about his son, and this was the final straw for Jane.

You were waiting at the front door that night, with a bag full of Hugh's clothes. Your wedding ring was missing from your finger, and your heart thumped so loudly against your chest I could hear it. I remember that evening very well.

Not least because of what happened before Hugh had had the chance to arrive home.

'Mum! Mum!' Jane could still hear the heartbreak in Malcolm's voice as he tugged at her arm, leading her into the living room where Edward was asleep by the fire.

Not asleep…

No. Not asleep.

It had been expected of course, but Jane hadn't dreamed that one of her own children might find their grandfather dead in his favourite chair. A loved one's impending death may loom for several years, but the hurt is still real when the time comes.

Hugh reacted with just enough empathy to delay Jane's request that he leave the house, but the wedding ring stayed off, and Hugh was made to sleep in another room in the house.

And we know which one he ended up in the most.

'She played with our *children!*' Jane exclaimed in the study. 'She laughed with them! Did homework with them! Treated them as though they were her own!'

Yes. I know. And one day, not long after the funeral, you finally made your move.

She said nothing to Hugh, but she deleted his phone number, changed the locks to the house, and boarded up the spare room that Rebecca had been using. Hugh stayed at the front door for three hours that night, but neither Jane nor the children said anything to him as they sat in Agnes' bedroom playing a board game together. Surprisingly, Hugh got the message and was never seen again.

Neither was Rebecca.

'No,' Jane said. 'Of course not. Why would you say that?'

The spare room Rebecca was using... It was the faraway one on the top floor, wasn't it?

'Yes,' Jane said, puzzled.

That's the "quiet room". The one you wouldn't hear a peep from. Three flights up and only the one door. I've always meant to ask you. Did you ever think to check inside before you boarded it up?

Jane said nothing. Her thoughts drifted to nothing for a few moments. Almost nothing.

Alright then. Where did we get to?

Two years went by faster than Jane would have liked them to. Malcolm had begun to struggle with emotions and was incredibly distant. He would refuse to talk about his father and Jane suspected difficulties at school. He was coming to the end of his studies there, and he had no clear idea of what he was going to do with his life when it was all over. He spent a lot of time outside the house when he could, but being so far away from everything else, Malcolm was forced to spend more time there than he would like. He took to spending long hours

WHICH WAY IS NORTH?

in the garden, away from everyone else. And Jane's relationship with him only deteriorated as time went on.

He told you he hated you one day, didn't he? And then you had a fight in the garden, shouting and screaming at each other. You were glad that you lived so far away from anyone else because if you had had neighbours, they might have been deeply concerned. Especially when you lost your temper completely and slapped Malcolm in the face. You might have been charged for that. Then one day he just up and left.

'No,' Jane corrected.

No? Oh, of course not! How silly of me to forget the order of things!

'Don't you have an ounce of empathy!?'

Sorry... Truly, I am.

It had happened on the windiest day Jane could remember for a long time. Agnes and Elise had been playing together. Elise had made a kite and was excited to see such a windy day. The girls took the kite out to the back garden, and Jane remembered hearing the excited laughter and being cheered by the sound of it. The sound of sheer horror and heartbreak that followed was something that would haunt Jane's sleepless nights for years to come.

A kite. Who would have thought a kite could be so dangerous? Elise had been flying it when the wind had a dramatic change of mind and sent it flying to the earth. It found the side of Agnes' head instead.

It wasn't your fault.

'No?' Jane enquired. 'It wasn't Elise's fault either, but that didn't stop her from falling into a state of irreparable mental ill health, did it? Do you know I haven't even spoken to her for... what? Sixteen, seventeen years now? I have no idea where she lives, whether she's single or has a partner, where she works, what kind of person she is. Nothing! I have nothing!'

Just like all your other children then.

'Oh, I hate you! I hate you!'

I know. You always have. Come now, finish the story. Whatever happened to Jacob?

Jacob lived in the city now. Jane had clung on to him, and he was the last to leave the family house by a long stretch. Elise had left aged eighteen, Jacob was thirty-three by the time his mother felt able to let go of him. She had tried desperately to get him to think about it, about how he would manage to live and work and form any relationships with his condition.

A mother who never let him grow up might have been worse for him though, Jane. Perhaps now he understands this. He hasn't been in contact for a long time, has he?

No. Jacob hadn't been in touch, and nor had anybody. The house had felt empty ever since Jacob left and this had allowed Jane's mind to perpetually ask all the "what if"s that it could think of.

What if she had picked a better man than Hugh?

What if you had never chosen to live in this house and let it fade, the wilderness around it finally enveloping it and hiding it from the world?

What if she had stood her ground and never allowed Rebecca a room?

What if your children could forgive themselves, and you?

'I know who you are now,' Jane mumbled, almost to herself.

Do you now? Good. Yes, that's good.

CHRIS MORRIS

What if she needn't be forever haunted by the ghost of a life unlived?

WHICH WAY IS NORTH?

I've Been Thinking Blue

She danced around His gloomy spirit like a happy bird whizzing elegantly above tall grass, embracing the refreshing feel of dew on Her feathers as She twirls just out of the reach of lurking vipers.

He spent the day staring at the wall and doing His best to convince Her that He was only half there; a pale ghost of a man, wandering grey, foggy streets in search of something swept up in secrecy. He was silent. As silent as that pale ghost, whose feet dared not drag the ground but softly sailed through the ether. And if She would dare to pull back the shroud that veiled His face, She would find a savage beast that would need little excuse to snap.

Notwithstanding, She thought She had Her ways of dealing with His mood. She knew what made men like Him tick, She deduced, and what made Him feel calm. This was not a foolproof system, and much care would need to be applied.

'I've been thinking blue,' She said. 'What do you think?'

He stared at the wall. Stared as though intending to melt a section to reveal the bones of it, a pressurised skeletal surrender in response to the heated wrath of its aggressor. He did not reply.

'Yes, blue,' She continued, regardless. 'A light kind, like a sky blue. It might brighten the place up, you know? Don't you think so?'

Looking at Him, She thought He hadn't even blinked. It was impossible to say whether He had heard Her and had chosen not to reply, or Her words had sailed through Him unnoticed like a cold breeze through bare, leafless branches hanging forlorn in winter.

'Or yellow,' She hopefully suggested. 'Instead of blue. Not a bright yellow. A custard, not lemon. I don't know. What do you think?'

He blinked once and spoke. 'Yes. Whatever you like.'

Vacant, uninterested, distracted by a mind filled with unhelpful notions and a turbulent sense of perturbation. *He's waiting,* She thought. *Waiting is bad for*

WHICH WAY IS NORTH?

Him. Especially with something like this. His mind is focussed on it, seething. He'd never admit it, but He's nervous. Maybe He can be distracted...

'Well if you're not going to be helpful, why don't we go for a walk, eh? Help take your mind off things?'

'He should have been here by now,' He said, removing His hard glare from the wall for a moment and swapping it to the floor. 'Where is he?'

'He said by the end of the day,' She said in a playful tone with an exacted chuckle. 'And we're hardly there yet, are we? Come on now, a nice little walk will do you good. It's a beautiful day.'

He stood up and walked to the window. 'I'm not leaving. I can't. He might come any moment now. You can go for a walk if you like.'

'That would hardly be professional now, would it?' She said, allowing a slight tone of deprecatory into Her voice.

He spun around from the window and faced Her, making eye contact for only the second time that day. He spoke quickly and with clear fury in His voice. 'Well why did you suggest it?'

She held Her breath. Their eyes might only have met for a few seconds, but it was enough for Her to see the demon partially masked within Him. She saw a vast, airless fire encircling a soul tortured by years of anguish and loveless despondency. The kind of uncaring and unvented spleen that would refuse to be halted by reason or sympathy. They were anomalistic eyes, the eyes of what some might call an unwaveringly determined man, and others a maniac. It was almost perfect really; He had the eyes of a –

Enough, She thought. *I've riled Him. Time to calm Him down.*

'All right,' She said. 'I was kidding about the walk. What about a cup of tea, though? We can see to that can't we?'

The fire in His eyes quenched somewhat, and He slumped back down to the chair on which He'd previously been sitting. The pale ghost returned. 'Not for me. You help yourself.'

She didn't argue. She strode the small steps to the kitchen area and filled the kettle before opening the first overhead cupboard She saw. Finding nothing there, She pulled the other one open, found what She needed and began the tea-making process.

As the kettle was boiling, She leaned on the counter and looked at Him. His back was facing Her, and He had resumed staring at the wall. She noticed that He was absently turning a small object around in His hands. She saw what it was and to Her scant surprise, felt a shiver of dull apprehension. The wait would be over soon enough. As the steam began to slowly escape from the kettle's outlet as though escaping the mad torment of the horrors within, She couldn't help but compare this kettle to Him. On the outside, an unreservedly ordinary thing. Unremarkable. But inside there was a hot storm infusing. One that, if left too long, might have a catastrophic conclusion. She wondered what had been His version of someone pressing a button.

But maybe that's just it. Your button was pressed. Who pressed it? And why?

And did they live to tell the tale?

She noticed now how dark the room was, as though this place ventured to conceal Him from the world like some dire, clandestine disgrace. Observing this, She could only imagine what iniquity lurked inside of Him; what was the unhappy consequence of His ignition, sparked by the press of His button?

She thought about asking His name. Stupid idea. Was He interested in Hers? Probably not. He wasn't interested in Her name or how She was feeling or who Her sister was dating or about the colours She was thinking about painting Her walls back home. He clearly had one thing on His mind; it was taking over any and all other thoughts, and would not be satisfied until this ghastly ordeal was completed. He could only think of –

He and She both jumped a little as there came a hurried, impatient knock on the door. Her mouth fell open as He turned to face Her, tightly gripping the arm of the chair. 'Get the door,' He said, and She wasted no time in following His command.

When She arrived at the door, She opened it confidently and with Her practised smile. Outside was a middle-aged man with thick brown hair and a very blank expression.

WHICH WAY IS NORTH?

That blank expression is as practised as my smile, She thought. *Anonymous, impartial. What else could you expect of a man like this?*

'Mr Phillips?' She asked warmly, and he nodded.

'May I come in?' Mr Phillips asked.

'Of course, come in, come in. We've been waiting for you. Beautiful day out there, isn't it? I might go for a walk later. I was just about to make a cup of tea. Would you like one?'

'Thank you,' Mr Phillips said, and stepped inside the lonely wooden cabin. 'It was quite difficult to find this place, you know. Oh, hello there, is this your associate?'

'Pleased to meet you Mr Phillips sir,' He said extending a hand intended to shake Mr Phillips', and with a cheery, wholesome smile on His face that looked so genuine that She was horrified. A sickly feeling came over Her then, and She decided to focus on the tea. She pulled another mug out of a cupboard, and as She discreetly wiped the dust from it and threw a teabag in, She contemplated the sheer needlessness of it.

She glanced at Him again, but only for a moment, not daring to let Her eyes linger on Him for any more than was necessary for fear of Her glimpse being scrutinised, not by *His* eyes but by His essence. By whatever it was that made Her feel like there were more than just He, She and Mr Phillips in the room. The idea of being discovered made Her feel a terror deep within Her that physically rattled Her. She looked long enough to gain a deeper understanding of His dramatic change to a person who seemed completely normal. Not just normal either, but charming, wholesome and even trustworthy. He was handsome, confident, and in His face She could see delicate rumours of a man with an eager and robust sense of humour. To allow Her mind to remain focussed on this absurdity would be to accept a pure form of horror into Her heart, so She turned away.

    He led Mr Phillips to a chair opposite the one He'd been sitting miserably on, and they began to exchange forced and phoney pleasantries that She was not particularly interested in hearing. She watched His face as He talked and marvelled in His ability to change so swiftly from a dark and foreboding force to a friendly and welcoming gentleman.

WHICH WAY IS NORTH?

She jumped when the water was boiled and the kettle loudly clicked off, thankful that neither He nor Mr Phillips had been looking in Her direction. She grasped for one of the mugs, Her hand knocking into it and making it wobble slightly before She caught it clumsily. As She lifted it, Mr Phillips, who had glanced over at the sound of the wobbling mug, sprang up from his chair.

'Where are my manners? Let me help you.'

Things happened both quickly and strangely slowly then. As Mr Phillips rose, She spotted His face, which had turned dark once more. The raging fire She'd observed before had returned, but now it was enough to melt the most courageous of hearts. Their eyes met again, and for a moment She was stunned by how much those eyes were able to articulately communicate exactly what He wanted Her to do, as though there was some other presence, able to talk to Her, separate from Him.

The kettle. Use the kettle.

And She did. She thumbed down the button to release the lid. It sprung open moments before She sent the contents of the kettle through the air and onto Mr Phillips' unsuspecting face, which quickly twisted into an expression of absolute agony as his thoughts no doubt suffered a brief moment of turmoil. His hands reached up to his hot, steaming face and he began to scream, but She knew this wouldn't last long: He was already on his feet. She was astonished to see that buried somewhere within the fire and fury of His face was a look of something like joy. It disturbed Her deeply.

    Having unquestionably had some experience with this type of situation, He already had His blade in hand. He raised it briskly to eye level before bringing it down on His target's back. She counted eleven strikes: four while Mr Phillips had still been standing, and a further seven as he lay defenceless on the ground. Each strike producing repellent amounts of blood, anguished sounds of a dying man, and enough venom and malice to bring down the most formidable of foes. One strike might have been enough, She thought, and then She shuddered, remembering that look of glee on His face as He'd stalked Mr Phillips from behind.

    When He was finished, He paused a moment above His victim. Leaving the knife where it was He stood, panting and looking down at the mess below Him.

WHICH WAY IS NORTH?

Something was different about Him. He seemed much more at ease. Was that a faint, satisfied smile hidden within His bleak face?

Something had changed in Her, too. Much of the anxiety and dread that had begun to hijack Her heart had quelled, and in its place was a cautious idea of hesitant peace. She still had the kettle in Her hand and noticing that She hadn't used all of the water, She flipped the lid shut again and poured the remains into one of the mugs She'd set on the counter.

'You sure you don't want one?' She asked.

CHRIS MORRIS

The Last Man Alive

From the journal of Harold Plumber:

I think I nearly died today. It was really close. Food was getting scarce, and although I've done well in these past few months to keep journeys to the supermarket and back to a minimum, I felt desperate. There's only so much I can take of a grumbling stomach, and besides, I need to keep energy levels as high as possible. You never know when one of – them – might give chase.

I've given up taking these trips under cover of darkness; I decided that the creatures have bad enough eyesight in the first place and it would do me much better to see my own surroundings with clarity when I'm off on one of my necessary travels.

I exited the bunker, quietly as always, and looking up and down the road, I saw no signs of life. It's been exactly three hundred and sixty-four days since I saw the last human. Jenny. She ran off into the darkness that horrible night and never came

WHICH WAY IS NORTH?

back. I have to assume she's gone. Gone like everyone else, to Armageddon, or the Rapture, or Doomsday, whatever you want to call it.

Oh, Jenny…

I saw no signs of the zombies on the way to the supermarket. Still, when I arrived, I swung the glass door inward carefully, because for some crazy reason there always seems to be some of them hanging around in there. I don't even look at them any more, not out of fear, but rather out of a desperate and stubborn refusal to accept their existence. Looking at them is a form of letting them win.

I wasted no time in collecting the usual tinned goods – soup, meatballs, vegetables. I packed them quickly and carefully into my backpack, being careful not to bash them together in a way that might attract attention. The shelves are still really full, even after all this time. This gives fuel to my belief that I really am the last of us all. The last of mankind.

As I was placing the last of the tins into my bag, I foolishly let my hand slip slightly and the tin went tumbling to the floor with a hard smack before rolling noisily underneath the shelf. I froze in place for what seemed like an eternity, waiting to see if I had attracted the attention of those vile things. After a few moments, I thought I was safe. I allowed myself to resume breathing. It was almost as though somebody was waiting for this because as soon as I let myself relax, I heard them — those familiar, groaning voices. From the sound of it, there were at least three of them. I knew I had to act quickly.

Without looking, I turned and sprinted for the door. I heard hurried footsteps behind me; in recent weeks they've been getting faster. Is it possible that they are evolving somehow? The groans became louder as I ran, and I could almost swear I could hear clear, comprehensible language coming from these creatures. It made me think, oddly enough of that old zombie film, the one where the zombies shout "Braaaaiiiinns". I know it's a comedy film, but it gave me the creeps nonetheless.

When I was out of the store, I ran full pelt without looking back. I heard one of the zombies crash through the door of the supermarket, and I quickened my pace. It shouted at me as I ran. I know that seems strange, but that's the only way I could satisfactorily describe it. My head has been playing tricks on me of late, and again I almost heard real words come out of the thing's mouth.

'Stoooop! Stoooop!'

WHICH WAY IS NORTH?

Am I going crazy with all this time alone? How long does it take for a man to go mad?

I'm going to get some rest now. I'm safe here in the bunker. I should be eternally thankful for that.

***

TO: Stephen.Boyd@SuperSavers.com
FROM: Michael.Alexander@SuperSavers.com
SUBJECT: Store Security

Dear Stephen,

It has been brought to my attention that once again, your store has been robbed by that same man. I am disappointed that I didn't hear this from you and that instead, I heard it "through the grapevine" from your colleagues, appropriately named Marvin.

You will recall, last month the same man entered the store you are responsible for armed with what looked like a golf club. He crouched, hidden among the shelves but of course our cameras picked him up. When he spied a local resident (an elderly lady leaning on a walking frame), he suddenly had a mad look on his face and raised the club above his head. If it weren't for Marvin interfering, I believe we could have had a very serious situation on our hands. We don't need any more negative media coverage after the out of date spam scandal.

After Marvin chased the man away, I think we were lucky that a six-pack of toilet paper and a box of SuperSave cereal were the only items he was able to snatch. Next time, he might grab the leftover spam and claim we're still selling it.

I would like you to reply to this email by close of business today with a full list of every item that this criminal got away with, and what your plans are for stopping this in future.

Regards,
Michael.

TO: Michael.Alexander@SuperSave.com
FROM: Stephen.Boyd@SuperSave.com

WHICH WAY IS NORTH?

SUBJECT: RE: Store Security

Dear Michael,

Thank you for your email. I'm sorry I didn't inform you sooner, and I'm ever so grateful that marvin managed to get in touch with you to inform you about the incident. I'm sure he appreciated how busy I've been and wanted to take the initiative to get in touch. I'll be sure to thank him. That's funny, I was just about to email you as well. Thank goodness for marvin.

The police were informed immediately, and I spent the day responding to their queries and assisting them. They were very grateful for the extra effort that I put in to help them find the man in question and in fact, one of them told me that my boss must be thrilled with me! I gave him your email address to pass this compliment on to you personally, but he said something about sometimes his emails don't work or something.

CHRIS MORRIS

I have this morning held a staff meeting in which I informed them of the incident, and I have asked them all to be more alert and vigilant. I'm not sure how many people were in when the last incident occurred, besides marvin, but I will find out and inform them all that they should have been much more watchful of the front door.

As for the list of items, from our stock check, it looks like the man got away with the following:

8x tins of SuperSave baked beans
10x tins of SuperSave soup
5x tins carrots
9x tins of SuperSave meatballs (out of date, but not by much!)
1x tin of alphabet spaghetti
3x multipacks of SuperSave cola
And another three boxes of that horrible cereal we sell. Nobody else buys that stuff, but this guy seems to like it.

On a final, unrelated note, we had a customer come in asking about a missing man, Harry I think she said. Her

WHICH WAY IS NORTH?

name was Jenny, but I forget her surname. I'm working closely with the police on this, and I will keep you informed.

Warm regards,
Stephen.

***

From *The Town Crier* newspaper:

LOCAL WOMAN SEEKING HELP IN TRACING MISSING MAN

A local woman is seeking help in tracing a missing man. Obviously. Because you've read the title of this article already and you know that, yet my boss always shouts at me whenever I fail to repeat the exact same information that you smart readers (if you were really that smart you wouldn't be buying THIS newspaper, that's for sure!) have just read. I'm glad that typing this stuff out helps me to release my inner frustrations and I'm thankful that I always remember to delete it afterwards before it goes to print. What a nightmare that would be! Haha. They'd probably fire me and replace me with Jimmy, who has the spelling and grammar skills of a five-year-old. Okay, I'll finish this crap later – tea break time.

A local woman is seeking help in tracing a missing man. Harold Plumber (22) was last seen during the incident which is now popularly being called the "ZATNW". His friend, Jenny Alexander (21), was the last to see him.

"I couldn't calm him down," she told *The Town Crier*. "He grabbed my hand and just started running. We got away safely from the ZATNW, and I was pretty sure that it was all over, but he kept saying 'No! No! I've been preparing for this! My granddad had a bunker we could use! I swiped the key from him years ago!' He was startled by something rustling in the bushes not long after and ran off on his own. I hope he's safe."

When asked if she had a message for Mr Plumber, Miss Alexander said: "Harry, if you're reading this, please rest assured that there is no danger out here. Come back to us. Should I say that nobody would blame him for hitting an old man in the face that he

WHICH WAY IS NORTH?

thought was... you know, *one of them?* Or would he be embarrassed about that? You know what, don't put that bit in."

Harold Plumber has been described as 5 ft 10, around 12 stone, and round glasses "like the ones Harry Potter wears". He had no facial hair on the night of his disappearance, but he may now be sporting a "thick, survivalist type" of beard.

***

TO: Stephen.Boyd@SuperSavers.com
FROM: Michael.Alexander@SuperSavers.com
SUBJECT: ...

Stephen,

This morning I received an email from one of your employees, Marvin. He has informed me that you have taken matters into your own hands regarding what you are describing as the "capture" of the problem thief. I shouldn't like to think that I need to remind you that hoisting one of our stock cages upside-down over the front entrance to the store is highly dangerous and should not be done in any situation. You said in your last email that you were working closely with the police – let them handle the arrest of this man.

I must also warn you that leaving a trail of SuperSave cereal which leads to a quiet area of the store where you intend to beat the culprit with a stale baguette is not an appropriate way to deal with this situation. You'll remember last year when we got complaints from one of our elderly customers, who complained that one of our "hard" baguettes was responsible for breaking his false teeth? I'd like to keep negative news about our baguettes out of the press, and beating somebody up with one won't achieve that.

Please give me a call when you have received this email. I look forward to discussing all of this with you.

Regards,
Michael.

***

From *The Town Crier* newspaper:

WHICH WAY IS NORTH?

WOMAN HOSPITALISED AFTER STOCK CAGE MYSTERIOUSLY FALLS "OUT OF THIN AIR" AT LOCAL SUPERSAVE

A women has been hospatalised after a stalck cage mysteereusly fell "out of thin air" at a local SuperSave store.

The Town Crier arrived at the seen shortly after, but we could only get the folowing short statment from managar Stephen Boyd:

"I don't know what happened. It just came out of thin air. Of course we don't keep cages roped up above the entrance to the store – we here at SuperSave pride ourselves on safety first and spam as fresh as a daisy as a close second. Rest assured I will find out who did this and the person responsible will be disciplined. Marvin! Do you know anything about this!?"

The women is said to be in a stabal condishon. *The Town Crier* will bring you more on this as the story un-fold's.

***

CHRIS MORRIS

TO: Stephen.Boyd@SuperSavers.com
FROM: Michael.Alexander@SuperSavers.com
SUBJECT: Call Me

Stephen,

I have tried calling you multiple times this morning. Call me as soon as you receive this email.

Michael.

***

Police Report of the arrest of Harold Plumber:

Police constable Richard Burns

    I attended the scene at the local SuperSave supermarket last Saturday, 12th July. When I arrived, I found the suspect, Harold Plumber, being held to the ground by a male member of staff. Mr Plumber was struggling against the staff member and could be heard shouting "Get off me! Get off me! Don't bite me! I don't want to turn into one of you!"

WHICH WAY IS NORTH?

The staff member could be heard shouting to his manager, later confirmed to be Mr Stephen Boyd: "Why are you just standing there!? Help me!"

Mr Boyd stood with a shocked expression on his face, and it appeared that his trousers were damp around the crotch area. He was very pale. I wondered if I should perhaps see if Mr Boyd needed medical assistance, but at this time I deemed the situation with Mr Plumber and the staff member more important.

Mr Plumber then bit the staff member, who could be heard screaming in agony. It was at this point, I intervened.

I placed handcuffs on the suspect while he could be heard saying: "They've got too smart! They've got too smart!"

The male staff member who had been bitten sat on the floor, and a substantial amount of blood could be seen coming out of his hand. While I restrained Mr Plumber, I asked Mr Boyd to assist his employee, at which point Mr Boyd fainted, knocking over a large display of half-price spam. I called for medical assistance at this point.

CHRIS MORRIS

At the station, Mr Plumber was placed in a cell while he continued to scream about an Apocalypse of some sort. Eventually, a woman named Jenny Alexander arrived at the station and was able to calm Mr Plumber down.

Nothing else to report about the arrest at this time.

***

From *The Town Crier* newspaper:

THE ZOMBIE APOCALYPSE THAT NEVER WAS: ONE YEAR ON

Today marks exactly one year since the dead rose from the grave. One year since there was "no more room left in hell, so the dead walked the earth". One year since we found out... that we were surprisingly well prepared for this.

Maybe it was the countless zombie movies or the perpetual preparedness for disaster that humanity always seems to display. But somehow, we were prepared. No sooner had zombies risen out of their graves had they been put back in them and told to stay

there, thanks in part to the army's eventual interference, but also thanks to the many who combatted the creatures armed with everything from baseball bats to frying pans.

Businessman Ryan Scott comments on that almost-fateful night:

"I was walking down the road when I saw a group of them. I just thought they were drunk at first, what with it being a Friday night. They staggered towards me, and I saw instantly that they were zombies: their flesh was all rotten and their eyes didn't look right. I don't know how they never seem to know in all those rubbish films. Anyway, I had just so happened to have been to my mate's house to have a look at his sink and I had a wrench on me, so I slammed it into their heads one by one, and they went down really easily. I mean, they were dead bodies, they weren't exactly strong or anything. Didn't hear a peep from any of the rest of them all night."

Scientists quickly discovered the chemicals used in the local cemetery's fertiliser was responsible (although many still theorise that chain supermarket

SuperSave's out of date spam was to blame). We interviewed gardener Danny Buchanan:

"I was just spraying the fertiliser as normal when suddenly a hand grabbed my leg. My first reaction was to shake it off and swear at the thing that grabbed me. Before I knew it, the body was rising up out of the earth. I would have been pretty scared if I wasn't caught up in the thought of 'how did it manage to get out of its coffin first?'. Anyway, I just so happened to have my rake on me, so I walloped the thing in the head. Went down easily enough."

Also in today's paper: interview with hero Marvin, who single-handedly incapacitated a mad robber at a SuperSave store. When asked how he knew the robber was coming, he was delightfully quoted as saying "I heard it through the grapevine!"

His manager, Stephen Boyd was approached for comment, but he declined.

CORRECTION: We published in one of last week's newspapers that the readers of *The Town Crier* are not smart. We'd like to once again reassure our faithful and well-educated* readers that this was an

WHICH WAY IS NORTH?

error written by a young man who was on work experience placement with us.

* there has been no official study into the intelligence, or lack thereof, of our readership.

CHRIS MORRIS

Caroline

This is the place where nightmares dwell
Where darkness reigns and terror fell.
In every part where dead things skulk
Deathly quiet, amassed in bulk.

They await the stranger from the skies
Hiding in the dark with an awful surprise.
Come one, come all, and do not fuss
Come see the man whose soul belongs to us.

And all around lie deserted homes
Where the wind does not whistle, but moans.

***

This is where those who have died an unspeakable death are doomed to forever wander in endless misery…

Every nook and cranny of this place stank of horror. In every corner, Sean could see blood, could hear screams, could smell death. He could feel the terror that clung to the walls like a creature of the deep sea wrapping its tentacles around its petrified victim as it drags it to the depths.

He vomited again. First time in a few weeks. He wondered if it was the memory of this place or the sickness that came with it. Or perhaps it was his own guilt, knowing that he had a major part to play in what had happened here.

He was in somebody's house. The person, or people who lived here did not know Sean, and he had never known them. But he knew important details about them, enough to know that he never wanted to meet them. He had feared deep inside that eventually there would come a time where he *must* encounter them. It had been one of the many, endless fears that kept him awake at night.

It hadn't taken long.

On his third night here, the *lady in red* came to visit him.

Or rather, *he* had visited *her*.

He had been the one that had invaded her house, after all.

He had been lying on top of a dirty mattress, watching the snow fall gently and soundlessly to the streets outside when he heard her footsteps. He was frozen to the bed in terror. His body went rigid, and it took a moment for him to even be able to turn his head towards the door of the bedroom he was in.

By the sound of the footsteps, he judged that whatever was coming was currently on the staircase. The old wood of the steps bent and creaked with each ghostly step.

He held his breath.

Outside the door, the footsteps stopped and were replaced by a slow scratching sound. The handle moved slightly and shakily as the thing behind the door fumbled with it, most likely trying to grasp on properly to push open. And then he heard what could only be described as a manic sort of moan.

'*Aaaaaaahhhhhhh! AAAAAAAHHHHHHH!!*'

Sean tensed his body. His eyes were wide circles beneath his sweating forehead.

And then the door opened. And there she stood. The lady in red.

WHICH WAY IS NORTH?

Only, she wasn't *wearing* anything red. Sean couldn't tell if she was really wearing anything at all. The red was unmistakably blood, appearing to pour all the way down the woman's body and soak the floor beneath her.

Sean screamed at the sight of her.

She screamed back.

Hers was a scream of haunting sadness mixed with unabated fury. It was enough to make Sean feel like throwing up. She stumbled into the room and began making awkward, jagged movements as she did so. She looked as though she was searching for something as her hands began patting the walls, leaving bloodied marks everywhere. She frantically searched the far wall and then stumbled, fell to the floor and crawled to another, all the while maintaining that desperate scramble.

And then she turned and faced Sean. Her face was scarred and burned. Several white blisters covered her dark, twisted face. Her eyes were fire; looking at Sean with a fury so deep it would have unsettled the most evil and unspeakable of demons.

His body finally allowed him to move when the lady sprung towards him. He shot up off of the mattress and flung himself out of the window, falling from the second floor and crashing into the thin layer of snow beneath. He pushed himself to his feet and sprinted down the empty streets without looking back, frantically patting away the snow on his body.

In the distance, the lady screamed.

He hadn't slept that night. He roamed the abandoned streets, trying to take some form of comfort in the gentle snowfall, but he could find none. He wondered for a moment why he didn't just allow himself to leave this place.

Because I shouldn't, was his answer. *If I leave, I shall be doomed to live a worse nightmare than even the one found here.*

He decided to spend each night in a different house. The change of scenery settled him somewhat, and he imagined it reduced his likelihood of another run-in with the red lady. He could picture her stumbling and dragging herself around each house, carefully checking every room for him. What exactly would she do with him when she caught him? His mind turned to every dark possibility imaginable. It made his very soul shiver.

The sickness had set in some two weeks later. He'd thrown up multiple times, and twice he found blood mixed in with the rest of the foul things ejecting from his body. His skin began to itch, lightly at first but eventually his arms, legs, neck and face were red and began to blister. By the third week, there was constant bleeding. He began to struggle to breathe, and when this eased off a little, it was no longer difficult, but incredibly painful. A consistent agonising cough began, and some of these again were accompanied by blood.

I've lost so much blood I should be dead already, Sean thought.

He'd been having nightmares of late; ever since he'd first learned of the impact of Caroline. He was mostly haunted by *her*, and the awful images in his head of her annihilation. And he couldn't help but compare himself to her because after all, he was more to blame than her for what had happened. When he dreamed of Caroline, he saw her in all her clear ugliness. Others would describe her as beautiful, as Sean would have before he arrived here. But now, every inch of her was weaved with sadness and distress. He dreamed that she could somehow walk, and as she did she would extend arms that were never there before outwards in an attempt to grasp him and drag him down to her own despair.

In another nightmare, he dreamed that it had stopped snowing. Outside he could hear an unfamiliar sound: joy and laughter. He peered out of the window (of a lovely, untouched and perfectly made-up bedroom) and he saw that outside the streets were filled with people, happily walking up and down, walking dogs, playing with children. This happiness was contagious, and Sean felt filled with it. It was as though Caroline had never happened at all.

Where is she now? She can't be here among all of this!

He threw on a coat and a pair of shoes and ran outside to meet with all of these hearty spirits. He whizzed down the stairs and swung open his front door. With a wide smile spread gleefully across his face he looked out -

- at the dead people on the ground.

WHICH WAY IS NORTH?

Every soul he had spotted outside of his window lay in front of him now in a horrific mess. Bodies were cluttered everywhere, some in disorganised piles and some in pieces, lying dejectedly alone. He found that sometimes his eye would catch the wide-open eye of one of the corpses and he couldn't bear to keep looking for more than a brief second.

Sean walked over to one of the bodies. A small boy. His eyes were closed, and remarkably, he had little sign of injury. Sean fell to his knees beside him, in grief. He began weeping and he started to feel sick again. And then the boy woke up.

He had black, frightened eyes and his mouth was missing all of his teeth. He had opened his mouth to speak, but Sean couldn't understand what he was saying. Eventually, he discovered that the boy was saying *help me*, before his black eyes and his body went still.

Sean wept all the harder and now took the boy in his arms and clutched on. He pressed his face against the boy's cheek and embraced him closely. He had woken up clutching on to a dirty pillow with a stain on it which painted a blurry image of the dark-eyed boy.

By the fifth week, Sean's nightmares were becoming unbearable. One night, after he finally fell asleep following a fit of bloodied coughs, he dreamed he was awoken by screams. He stood up and ran outside his house. When he flung the front door open, the screams got louder but nobody was there. He called out to the ghostly, invisible people, but nobody answered. He ran down the empty streets, and as he did the screams continued escalating in volume. They got so loud that he covered his ears with his hands in a failed attempt to cut the noise out, for it was louder still when his hands were at his ears. He took them away from his head and looking down at them, he saw that there were thousands of tiny, terrified faces on his hands screaming loudly.

Suddenly the sky lit up in a huge beam of radiant brilliance. The light seemed to make Sean's scars burn badly, and it was too much for his eyes which he now tightly shut and placed an arm over her forehead to try to block out some of the pain. The little people on his hands howled louder than ever as Sean cried out the only word that was on his mind. The name that haunted his every waking moment.

WHICH WAY IS NORTH?

'Caroline!!!'

Finally, the light faded to darkness, but the faces continued to shout and now Sean joined in on the wailing. Every single face was staring at him, wide-eyed and petrified. They seemed afraid of *him*. He pleaded with them to stop screaming, but they wouldn't. He felt as though it was driving him to madness.

He felt he had to do something about it.

He ran into the nearest house and found the kitchen. Inside one of the drawers, he took out the sharpest knife he could find and placed his hand face down on the counter.

The faces on his left hand began crying out and pleading.

No! Please! Don't cut us off!

You can't do this!

Please!!!

Sean ran the blade back and forth across the top of his left wrist. The pain was searing, but he continued madly slicing into his skin while the red faces of the people on his hand continued moaning in horror. He eventually passed out.

And when he awoke in the same house, with the same scarlet knife in his hand and no faces but a new, deep gaping wound in the top of his wrist, he realised that it was no dream at all…

After that, the sickness seemed to disappear. The vomiting stopped, his breathing was clearer, and the sight of blood had not been present for several days, save for the wound on his wrist. He'd wrapped his hand in toilet paper temporarily until he'd found some proper bandages two days later. He found nothing else to treat his wound with however, and it stung and throbbed painfully. He should have had enough bandages to keep replacing the old ones with for about a week, but the bleeding was so severe that they were soaked within minutes.

Why am I even bothering to bandage it up? Sean found himself wondering. *Why not just bleed out and end all of this?*

Because you need to see it all. You need to see Caroline's destruction. You need to understand fully the extent to which she ruined lives.

Why? I've seen enough!

WHICH WAY IS NORTH?

No. You can linger here in this place for a thousand years, and still you would not know the terror and utter desolation that she caused. You could never know it. And that's why they hate you.

Sean knew that "they" hated him for more than the simple reason of being unable to understand or appreciate their pains. They hated him because of much more than that. Oh yes. If they could, they would drag him down with them into the very depths of their despair to show him, just for a moment, what the word "pain" really meant. They would tear his very *being* from him, crumple it up and throw it into the nothingness beyond what was waiting for them. And even then, he would know nothing of their everlasting anguish.

He was eventually visited again.

This time it was a pale spectre of a being. He'd been unable to sleep and was staring out of the window at the falling snow (oh, why was he still pretending to himself that it was snow?), when he heard a noise coming from the bathroom. A slight bump followed by what sounded like soft weeping. Shivering, Sean got out of bed and walked quietly down the hall and stood outside the bathroom door.

Undeniably, something was in there, and it was crying.

The sobs were soft and delicate. They depicted a great, hopeless sadness. It sounded to Sean like the most fragile, melancholy music that one would hear and be compelled to switch off for fear of being dragged into the same depression that the music was born from. For a moment, he was unafraid and stuck in his own grief. So much so, that some tears of his own began to form in his eyes.

He wanted to see this person. The bathroom door was open a mere fraction, just enough to let out a thin strip of light if there had been one on inside. He carefully placed the fingertips of his right hand on the door and gently pushed.

The door creaked loudly.

It opened just far enough for Sean to see the figure at the other side of it spin round and face him, less than two feet away. Through the thin gap in the door frame, he could see a terrified face. He didn't know whether it was male or female, old or young. It was as pale as the light shone from a full moon but where its eyes should have been there were two large, black holes. Its mouth was much larger than it should have been for the size of its head, and it twisted into a shocked and scared expression. Like the lady in red, it screamed. But there was no anger in this scream, no fury. It was the terrified wail of someone that feared for their life.

The last sounds of its life, no doubt.

It pulled the bathroom door fully open, and Sean jumped back. The thing moved swiftly out of the room crying and screaming, never taking its huge black eyes from Sean. It floated down the hallway and disappeared.

Sean was frozen stiff, listening out for the spectre and wondering where it might have gone. The hallway was too dark to see anything in much detail, and it was impossible to know which way it went. Deciding that the thing clearly didn't want anything to do with him, he walked slowly back to the bedroom. Upon opening the door, he found it there, sitting on his bed.

It shot its head up upon Sean entering the room and wailed once more in terror. Once more, it flew past him and disappeared. Sean decided to try a different house for the night, remembering that the lady in red had not followed him, but it was no good. Each house Sean visited, the spectre was there, screaming in terror in sight of him. He tried sleeping in one of the houses that the spirit had fled from, but peculiarly, it kept coming back into his room, seeing him and fleeing in terror again. Its screams were the most unpleasant sound that Sean had ever heard. It would be a while, he thought, before he felt safe enough to sleep again.

Ultimately, the sickness returned. The nausea, the bleeding, the difficulty breathing. But this time it was more severe. Sean felt as though his time was nearly up. He felt exhausted all the time. Everywhere he walked, he left blotches of blood in the "snow" below his feet.

But finally, he found what it was he was looking for. It came in the form of a little girl.

She stood around four feet tall. Her clothes were ragged – full of holes and tears of every shape and size, revealing a dark, scarred skin, a mixture of black and deep scarlet. She had no hair, and a face so deformed that it was impossible to see anything that resembled human expression. A hideous set of dark, crooked teeth were revealed by lips that had somehow been pulled back or ripped away. One eye was missing, and the other was swollen to the point where it seemed as though it might burst upon the slightest of touches. Her nose with nothing more than two deep slits in the middle of her head.

'It's you!' Sean wailed. 'Caroline!'

She moved slowly towards him, every painful step coming awkwardly and painfully. Sean could almost feel the endless agony of every movement.

She extended an arm out to him and only then did Sean notice that three of her fingers were missing. Minimal casualties of a much greater struggle. The hand limply fell onto Sean's cheek, and the girl stood, crookedly staring into Sean's face.

The two of them stood there for a moment, looking at each other. And then the girl spoke.

'You... Did this...'

It sounded almost like a question, and Sean nodded bleakly because he could not work up the courage to speak any more.

'Caroline...' the girl croaked.

And finally, Sean broke. Tears streamed down his face, and he wailed in anguished despair, just like the pale spectre as the girl stood, disfigured arm still holding on to his cheek. He wept for what seemed like a long time, and then the girl collapsed to the floor, limp. Sean picked her up and carefully cradled her in his arms. She was as light as a dark, ghostly shadow. He carried her out of the burned ruins of the house he was in, outside to be softly buried in the greyish white falling from the stars above.

As he walked out of the house and into the road outside of it, he continued to weep. Just ahead of what used to be the gate of the house, one of the girl's arms dropped and then snapped off like a twig, hitting the floor with a thud. Sean lowered the girl beside it then bent onto his knees and wailed into the darkness.

'Caroline! It was me who dropped you! I am the bringer of your destruction! I confess! *I confess!!*'

And as though in answer, the streets became swarmed with many dark creatures that had been hiding. The lady in red and the terrified pale spectre were there among thousands of others, all of them looking to be in similar pain to anyone else. Scarred and blackened faces, missing limbs, faces so deformed that if Sean were to survive this, would haunt his every moment of life henceforth. As they moved in towards him, they began whispering and moaning:

'Caroline! Caroline! Carooooline!!!'

And finally, they reached him, and Sean let them take him. At first, he did not know what word to use to describe what was happening to him, but around three seconds before his death, he thought of the perfect word to describe it.

Devoured.

***

We saw a man come wandering
His heart was sore, his face was grim
Lost he was, and murmuring
So then we went and ate him

CHRIS MORRIS

50/50

Alex closed her eyes.

The news was too much. She'd spent five days on this god-forsaken ship hearing bad news, but this was just extreme.

'And you really can't tell me anything else?' she asked, without being able to look at the monitor in front of her to see Mike's face. 'You can't tell me which one he went for?'

She heard Mike sigh. 'Alex, I would tell you if I knew myself. I don't have a clue. I can see him here, frozen with his eyes closed. Everything looks normal, but I don't know how long he's chosen to be out for.'

Damn it. Damn his stubbornness, damn this place, damn everything. Alex found herself, hardly for the first time, wishing that she was back home. Back on Earth.

'Okay,' she said to Mike, opening her eyes again and looking at him. He had a genuine sympathetic expression on his face, and it both comforted and hurt

WHICH WAY IS NORTH?

Alex. 'Thanks for trying to check anyway. I know our ships are both supposed to be... You know, not doing this sort of thing for each other.'

'Don't be daft, Alex,' Mike said. 'You're an old friend.'

'Well,' Alex said. 'Thanks again.' She reached for the "END SIGNAL" button, but she was stopped.

'Hang on a second,' Mike said.

'What is it?' Alex asked.

'What are you going to do?' Mike asked. He looked deeply concerned.

Alex turned away from the monitor again and sighed. 'I'm going under. Tomorrow.'

'How long for?' Mike asked.

'I don't know,' Alex replied. 'I've got a fifty per-cent chance of getting it right.'

'And a fifty per-cent chance of getting it wrong,' Mike pointed out.

Obviously, Alex thought, irritatedly.

'Listen,' Mike said. 'You know I'm gonna have to make my choice really soon too. I could let you know right now what it'll be. Then at least you'll have one old friend.'

Alex looked back at the monitor. She was moved by this, but she knew she must refuse. 'Thanks Mike, but I can't make my decision right now. I've got to think about it.'

'Yeah,' Mike said softly with a nod. 'Yeah, of course.' There was a moment's pause. 'Well, if I don't see you… have a good life.'

'Yeah,' Alex forced a smile. 'You too, Mike. Goodbye.'

The screen went black.

***

Alex was a part of what was being called the "great exodus" among what she deemed the more dramatic type of people from Earth. The sun had been expanding faster than humans had at first anticipated, and the planet was quickly becoming uninhabitable. Many older people, or those with pre-existing health conditions had sadly died, and the time had come for the human race to launch full pelt into interplanetary colonisation.

WHICH WAY IS NORTH?

Several ships had set out from Earth and the population there was now next to nothing. Alex's ship, *The Spacehawk* had set out alongside one other, *Columbus*. The two planned to fly side by side all the way to their two destinations: planets several light-years apart that scientists had had strongly suspected could support human life for many centuries to come.

Years ago, when a "great exodus" such as this one had first been suggested, the general opinion around Earth had seemed to be that it was pure madness. The closest planet outside of our own solar system that had potential for colonisation was hundreds of light-years away. Any people sent on a mission there would have died before they reached it, even if the problem of being unable to have a limitless quantity of food, water and oxygen was somehow resolved.

And then they finally cracked it. Perfect stasis. Freezing a person safely for what was before an unimaginable length of time, and having them awake at the end of it. It was perfect. Human beings could travel for hundreds, maybe even thousands of years through space in what would seem the blink of an eye. No need for food, water, oxygen. Close your eyes one end and open them at the other. Easy.

The passengers of *The Spacehawk* and *Columbus* were given two options. They could go into stasis for one hundred years, and awake at the planet named Athena. From what scientists could see, Athena was a beautiful, Earth-like planet which was free from pollution and enjoyed long summers and short winters. Natural resources on the planet seemed to outnumber those left on Earth, and humans had the chance, if they would take it, to make this planet a wondrous, green, beautiful place to be enjoyed for many, many centuries.

The other choice was to go into stasis for two hundred years, to a planet twice the length away from Earth called Poseidon. This was a planet roughly the size of Jupiter, but it was around eighty per-cent ocean. Interestingly, scientists had strong reason to believe that there was life on this planet on the lands as well as the oceans. Nothing was confirmed, but the idea of discovering completely new life and the first outside of their home planet of Earth was appealing enough to people that they chose this planet immediately, despite

WHICH WAY IS NORTH?

the one week aboard the ship that was labelled the "decision period".

For a long time, neither Alex nor her boyfriend Craig could make their minds up about where it was they wanted to end up. Eventually, they had decided. But this caused another problem altogether.

'You'd give up the chance of being among the first people to discover *aliens*, just so you can attempt to build a Utopia on a planet that's just as boring as this one?' Craig had asked, bewildered, two days before the ships were due to take off.

'Oh come on,' Alex had complained. 'There's only a *chance* that there's life over on Poseidon. It's pretty *certain* that Athena is just beautiful. And we can keep it that way. You know, there could even be life there too. Less of a chance than on Poseidon, but still a chance.'

'You really think the human race – *our* lot can actually keep that planet from going the same way Earth did? Don't be stupid!'

Stupid!? Had he really called her stupid?

That had set her off. She'd walked out on him, and then the whole same routine played out again. She slammed a door. He grumbled something from behind it. She began to wipe a tear out of her eye while cursing the fact it was even there. He went silent. She tried to occupy herself with something else. He eventually called or messaged to say he was sorry. She gave a short, in-the-middle type of response because she couldn't decide how she felt about the situation. They eventually kissed and made up.

And waited for the whole thing to start again.

'Fine,' Craig had said. 'Fine, we'll go to your Athena.'

'No,' Alex had stubbornly said. 'You'll make me feel bad for the rest of my life for making you miss out on your aliens. We'll go to Poseidon.'

'This is totally unfair!' Craig had wailed. 'You're only doing that to make me feel horrible! Like I'm the complete dickhead that will make you miserable for the rest of your life while you watch the people on Athena through a TV screen having the time of their lives!'

Alex had screamed then. 'Why do you have to make everything so fucking difficult!?'

WHICH WAY IS NORTH?

'*Me!?*' Craig had shouted, disbelievingly. 'I'm trying to give you what you want! I'm telling you we'll go to your planet and *I'm* the one making things difficult? Do you hear yourself!?'

The slammed door. The grumble from the other side of it. The stupid tear that didn't have to be there. The silent treatment. The attempt to put it out of her mind.

The attempt to put it out of her mind…

The attempt…

Where's the message? Where's the phone call?

Alex had taken out her phone and checked the last time Craig had been on. Two minutes ago. What was he up to? Why hadn't he apologised? Should *she* apologise?

Hell no.

She'll wait. And eventually the same old *I'm sorry, I was a total dick, I love you, you deserve better from me* spiel would come, and she wouldn't know how to respond to it.

She waited. It didn't come.

Looking at her phone screen, a rush of anger flushed through Alex.

We're leaving tomorrow. Tomorrow! And he doesn't want to speak to me? I can't believe this. How could he do this to me? I guess this trip on the ship is going to be fun then.

He'll message.

He won't message! He hasn't messaged!

He always does, though.

Not this time. You know what? I don't even want to go on the ship with him any more. I wish I could go on a completely different...

***

It was probably a rash decision, Alex had eventually concluded two days into the journey aboard *Columbus*. She'd called Sarah, one of the organisers she'd known quite well to enquire about the possibility of switching ships. As it had happened, she'd had a gentleman call her up the day before, asking about the same thing but the other way around. Easy solution – Alex could swap with the man who was supposed to be on *Columbus*.

She'd let anger take her. She told herself she didn't regret it, but she knew she was afraid to admit to herself that she should have sucked it up and spoken to Craig.

WHICH WAY IS NORTH?

Her mind got caught up in determination to be the one who was *right* in the argument. It was stupid.

Still, Alex and Craig had had no contact with each other, and she had barely thought about what her decision was going to be in regards to how long she would be in stasis and which planet she would end up on.

Just call him. Are these stupid arguments enough to warrant never seeing each other again?

No. He should call me. He's the one that started it.

You're the one that walked away.

Shut up.

God, I'm just fighting with myself now.

By day four, she had begun to feel anxious.

She stared out of the window at breakfast, trying to be awed by the epic vastness of space outside. She should be; she should be absolutely stunned by the view. But her mind couldn't stop wondering about Craig. Was he thinking about her? Was he angry at her? Did he miss her?

Was he already in stasis?

No! He wouldn't do that! He would surely call before he did so, informing Alex about what his decision was so that they could be together and spend their lives exploring a brand new world.

Unless he was too angry.

Why would he be angry? Her own anger had diluted now, had almost completely vanished. She found that she missed him deeply and that the fighting was all just foolish. They were stressed – they were about to leave their whole world behind them, and they had a huge, life-shaping decision in front of them to make. Of course they were going to argue if they didn't find a way of getting their stresses externalised in a non-aggressive way.

She started to look forward to speaking to him again.

***

'Craig's already in stasis,' Mike had said.

And the words rang out and echoed in her mind all night long.

Craig's already in stasis…

Craig's already in stasis…

Already in stasis…

WHICH WAY IS NORTH?

Already...

***

Alex stepped inside the chamber.

'Okay,' Jane, the ship's stasis chamber officer said with a smile. 'Lie down comfortably. Place your hands gently against your stomach, and when you're ready I'll close the door. Once I do so, close your eyes. You'll be frozen, and you'll wake up many years from now, but it will just feel like you've slept for one night, as usual. Now, could you please confirm how many years you are going into stasis for?'

Alex had internally debated this for a long time. She'd barely slept the night before. She'd arrived at an idea early on that she could choose to sleep for one hundred years and wake up in Athena. She could search for Craig, but if he wasn't there she could ask to go under for another hundred years. It seemed like the perfect plan until she was told that a person could not go back into stasis so quickly after doing it the first time.

Damn.

Then she thought about asking Mike to leave a note on Craig's chamber. But what good would that do?

Hi Craig, it's me, Alex. I'm sorry we had a fight. I love you and I want to be with you. If you're reading this after a one/two hundred year sleep...

It didn't fix anything.

What was he most likely to choose? He had wanted to take the two hundred year option and fly to Poseidon for a chance at discovering alien life. If he had been angry with Alex when he went under, then that would most likely still be his position. Or maybe he'd gone through something similar to Alex and was feeling guilty about the fight. Maybe then he had chosen to take the one hundred year sleep and go to Athena.

Oh, this was impossible...

She began to think about which of the two worse case scenarios was less distressing. To wake up after one hundred years only to find Craig still asleep, and for the rest of your life frozen and floating away to a planet an unreachable distance away? Or to wake up after two hundred years to find that Craig is dead after having lived a life far away from you which you were no part of? She decided this. She didn't know whether she would see Craig again. But she could do something for herself. She could choose to go where her heart desired. And then at least if she missed Craig, she would have given herself the gift of living on the planet *she* had wanted to live on.

'Alex?' Jane asked. 'What is your choice?'

'One hundred years,' Alex said confidently. 'I'm going to Athena.'

***

The experience was exactly as Jane had described it. Alex lay in the chamber as comfortably as she could, and she shut her eyes when the door closed. She heard some beeping and then a sudden rush of cold air before everything went dark.

One hundred years and one heartbeat later, she began to stir. The chamber felt warmer now. Had she really slept for a century? She was afraid that somehow she'd misinterpreted and so lay there for a few moments, wanting to be more sure that the time had come.

She thought of Craig. She wondered whether he was awake or asleep. Her heart began beating more rapidly, and she realised how much she desperately hoped that he had chosen the same option as her.

A familiar voice interrupted her thoughts.

'Alex? You can open your eyes. Your stasis is over.'

The voice of Jane, who had no doubt awoken from her own stasis not long before Alex.

Craig… are you here? Are you awake? I'm ready to put the stupid fights behind us and enjoy this beautiful new world together.

Alex opened her eyes.

WHICH WAY IS NORTH?

Passing Places

Dear Mirryn,

You came into this world quietly and curiously. I was the first person you saw. The look on your face was one I still see to this day; that distant leer, with a surface of uncertainty which isn't just youthful naivety. It's also a desperate endeavour to seem *belonged*. A cry out to the universe for acceptance. It's a look of someone trying to find their way in the wide world. I know the look, and the feeling all too well.

Your little eyes met mine for just a second but held on for moments longer. I loved you the instant I saw you, and I felt even then that you were comforted by my presence, new and confusing as it was. I don't know what you saw in my face, but I imagine it was a slow, sure change from an expression of daunting perturbation to that of fleeing, unyielding joy.

And when I held you for the first time – when I held my little girl in my arms... I felt happiness, yes, but something else too. A great weight. One that seemed placed there by an imposing entity of some sort, which would no doubt ease off as the months and years went by, and I found the correct pair of shoes to fit my new father's feet as I confidently walked the path of parenthood.

But the path, which I guilelessly saw as somewhat straight with the slightest of bumps here and there, turned out to be rather different. And the weight that was placed on me did not get lighter, but significantly heavier as the years pressed on.

I'd always imagined my parenthood as a combined effort of multiple positive influences. I would take care of your most prominent needs first, and then I would teach you to sing and dance, paint and colour, laugh and make music. Whenever you would fall I would pick you up and wipe away the debris, and always when I didn't know the best course of action, there would be external aid: other influences which could support me, and us. But Mirryn, sometimes things don't work out the way we think they will.

WHICH WAY IS NORTH?

I know you see your father as a brave warrior. A man who is not afraid of anything. Monsters that prowl the night would come across his house and flee in terror when they caught scent of whose door they had come wickedly sniffing at. All shall respect your father and fear him.

But the truth is, Mirryn, I'm scared. I am afraid, and I always have been.

I know you don't understand this. There are a great many things that are difficult for me to explain to you, and to myself for that matter.

I think of how far you've come, but I fear how far you have yet to walk on a path that is veiled by fog so thick that it is itself another obstacle on your journey. I imagine myself holding your little hand through as much of this as I can, until it gets so big that one day I shall hold it for the last time and let go, not knowing that I will never feel the touch of it again. And then where will you be? What part of the path will you be on and how much fog will there be? And will you wander off, looking for an answer to that distant leer that's been with you from the beginning? And will you find it? And how heavy will my weight, and my heart feel then?

When I found myself alone with you, the weight had never felt heavier. As I walked the path of fatherhood, I found that it sloped sharply upwards and became dizzyingly steep. As I climbed, I dared not look upwards for fear of seeing it become unscalable. But what then, Mirryn? What happens to us if that path becomes too treacherous to navigate?

I do not know the answer to a great many things, but I believe I have found the answer to this.

I write this letter to you as you sleep, undisturbed by the maddening thoughts that haunt my waking life. I am writing it for you, but also somewhat to myself. To remind myself of just how possible it is to traverse the paths of parenthood when you have your passing places. When the road ahead becomes distinctly turbulent, a passing place can help ease the journey and make the way less perilous.

Yesterday we made an autumn wreath.

'What's a wreath?' you asked.

WHICH WAY IS NORTH?

'Like the Christmas one we put on our door,' I said.

'What's an autumn one?' you asked.

'One made out of the colourful autumn leaves,' I said.

'Cool,' you said.

We took a walk in the woods looking for the most beautiful fallen leaves that we could find. You excitedly picked out the biggest and most colourful ones and placed them in the plastic zip bag we took with us. You said you could smell the autumn in the air and you told me it was now your favourite season. I laughed. You asked why. I said "nothing" while thinking that you would likely say the same of winter after we visit Santa.

When we got home, we glued the leaves to a grapevine wreath I had bought, and we hung it up on our front door. You got glue all over your hands, and we had to scrub it off with warm soapy water that smelled of strawberries. When your hands were dried, you ran out to see the front door and you admired the beauty that we, father and daughter had created together. You didn't see it, but I quickly wiped a tear out of my eye. If you'd caught it and asked me why it was there, I'd have said something like "Sometimes people cry when they're really happy". And you would accept this answer, baffling as it would be, but for myself, I'd have an even less clear answer for why a tear was there.

The next morning you ran out to see your wreath once again and found that the leaves had curled up and gone more brown. The beautiful colours were lost, and I saw that look in your face again; the distant leer. My heart somewhat sank, but I had an idea. After breakfast, we drove to the craft shop and we bought some construction paper. We drew leaf shapes onto the brown, red and golden pieces, cut them out and folded them into three-dimensional autumn leaves to replace the real discoloured ones on our wreath. We sprinkled these with the extra ingredient we'd purchased from the shop – gold and silver glitter. Our elderly neighbour Agnes came out to shower you with praise.

'Oh my, what a *beautiful* wreath!' she beamed. 'You've given me such a lovely view from inside my kitchen window!'

WHICH WAY IS NORTH?

You smiled, and for a moment it seemed our treacherous paths were almost forgotten, demystified and decorated with all the colours of autumn leaves.

And it's days like these, Mirryn, that help that sloping path of mine begin to flatten just a little, and the weight to feel less than it is. And onwards we march together through the passage, my father shoes feeling fresh and tightly secured, for now at least. I have found that there is not just one pair of father shoes, but many. Today they are made from construction paper and glue, but tomorrow they may be made from marbles or storybooks, and they must be changed often to make sure the path is still walkable.

As you sleep I look through the pictures I took of you making the wreath, and I smile, but that peculiar tear forms in my eye once more, and this time transforms into rivers of emotion flowing down my cheeks.

Why?

I believe it is a combination of happiness and of the intense, overwhelming emotion associated with that weight that was placed on me when I met you for the first time: the one that is ever-growing. Being your father is a tough job, Mirryn. You are a sweet, joyful, happy and caring child, but I am a man who is perpetually haunted by nightmares of what might be if I fail you, if I let your hand slip and lose you in the fog, the last thing I see on your face being not the leer but a look of disappointment. That, Mirryn, is what I fear most.

But for all the tears, days like these are important for me. Today was a passing place, a place for us both to take a short break and rest to find the next day that our paths have become a little easier. Passing places are found in craft days, visits to castles, walks in the park, film nights, drives in the countryside and baking cakes. They are the moments that I find I can forget about my weight and move ahead with you cheerfully, and be that brave warrior that you think I am, and watch you grow to be the brave warrior that I *know* you are.

For all the exhaustion of helping you walk your path, I am both bewildered and awe-inspired to see how easy it is for you to help your father walk his. For every moment of self-doubt, there is a reassuring smile. For every worry that your hand is slipping from mine, there is a squeeze from yours. You are my hero, my little saviour, for without you my path would perhaps be freer from obstacles, but profoundly darker. You are the light by which I can see enough to navigate my way through life.

And each night after I kiss your cheek and say goodnight I close your door, take the deepest of breaths and with both a tear and a smile I tell myself: 'You can do this.'

And the weight eases.

CHRIS MORRIS

About the Author

Chris Morris has been writing for as long as he can remember, but decided to start sharing his writings with the world in 2020. He lives in Dundee, Scotland with his young daughter, Mirryn.

Chris writes and produces a weekly podcast called *Short Stories by Chris Morris* which is available on all major podcast platforms. His first book, *Which Way is*

WHICH WAY IS NORTH?

North? released in November 2020, and he has plans for more books (including longer stories) in 2021.

When he's not writing fiction, Chris works as a pupil support assistant in a high school, and teaches drum kit and percussion at Dundee Drum Academy, a business he has been running since 2011.

For all the latest on Chris, follow him in these places:

facebook.com/ShortStoriesByChrisMorris
twitter.com/chrismorris1982
www.chrisamorris.com

Printed in Great Britain
by Amazon